He had just about everything she'd ever wanted in a man.

He was smart, thoughtful, sexy. Caring. If only she could convince him to give them a chance.

Wait a minute.

Why couldn't she convince him? At least try to convince him? He'd told her all he was interested in was a fling. And he'd backed off the moment she'd told him she wanted more. But just because he'd backed off didn't mean she had to.

Convincing him to give them a chance wouldn't be easy. He had his head wrapped around his crazy goal as tightly as any man hanging on to a lacerated heart. Breaking through all that would be tricky. And if she didn't pull it off, it was going to hurt.

But if she won…

Dear Reader,

Celebrate those April showers this month by curling up inside with a good book—and we at Silhouette Special Edition are happy to start you off with *What's Cooking?* by Sherryl Woods, the next in her series THE ROSE COTTAGE SISTERS. When a playboy photographer is determined to seduce a beautiful food critic fed up with men who won't commit…things *really* start to heat up! In Judy Duarte's *Their Unexpected Family,* next in our MONTANA MAVERICKS: GOLD RUSH GROOMS continuity, a very pregnant—not to mention, single—small-town waitress and a globe-trotting reporter find themselves drawn to each other despite their obvious differences. Stella Bagwell concludes THE FORTUNES OF TEXAS: REUNION with *In a Texas Minute.* A woman who has finally found the baby of her dreams to adopt lacks the one element that can make it happen—a husband—or *does* she? She's suddenly looking at her handsome "best friend" in a new light. Christine Flynn begins her new GOING HOME miniseries—which centers around a small Vermont town—with *Trading Secrets,* in which a down-but-not-out native repairs to her hometown to get over her heartbreak…and falls smack into the arms of the town's handsome new doctor. *Least Likely Wedding?* by Patricia McLinn, the first in her SOMETHING OLD, SOMETHING NEW… series, features a lovely filmmaker whose "groom" on celluloid is all too eager to assume the role in real life. And in *The Million Dollar Cowboy* by Judith Lyons, a woman who's fallen hard for a cowboy has to convince him to take a chance on love.

So don't let those April showers get you down! May is just around the corner—and with it, six fabulous new reads, all from Silhouette Special Edition.

Happy reading!

Gail Chasan
Senior Editor

Please address questions and book requests to:
Silhouette Reader Service
U.S.: 3010 Walden Ave., P.O. Box 1325, Buffalo, NY 14269
Canadian: P.O. Box 609, Fort Erie, Ont. L2A 5X3

THE MILLION DOLLAR COWBOY

JUDITH LYONS

Silhouette®

SPECIAL EDITION®

Published by Silhouotto Books

America's Publisher of Contemporary Romance

SILHOUETTE BOOKS

ISBN 0-373-24680-3

THE MILLION DOLLAR COWBOY

This edition published by arrangement with Harlequin Books S.A.

® and TM are trademarks of Harlequin Books S.A., used under license.
Trademarks indicated with ® are registered in the United States Patent
and Trademark Office, the Canadian Trade Marks Office and in other
countries.

Visit Silhouette Books at www.eHarlequin.com

Printed in U.S.A.

Books by Judith Lyons

Silhouette Special Edition

Awakened by His Kiss #1296
Lt. Kent: Lone Wolf #1398
The Man in Charge #1462
Alaskan Nights #1547
A Texas Tale #1637
The Million Dollar Cowboy #1680

JUDITH LYONS

lives in the deep woods in Wisconsin, where anyone who is familiar with the area will tell you one simply cannot survive the bitter winters without a comfortable chair, a cozy fireplace and a stack of good reading. When she decided winters were too cold for training horses and perfect for writing what she loved to read most— romance novels—she put pen to paper and delved into the exciting world of words and phrases and, most important of all, love and romance. Judith loves to hear from her readers. You can contact her through her Web site at www.judithlyons.com.

For my daughter, Chloe, who knows
that keeping one's feet on the ground is a good,
responsible, *important* thing to do. *But*...who also knows
the best view is from the clouds—and that the truly
clever person can do both. Keep flying high, sweetie,
and remember *always* that you are loved.

Chapter One

He had the saddest eyes she'd ever seen, and the sexiest smile this side of the Rio Grande.

Considering Josie Quinn was in a small honky-tonk in Texas, "this side of the Rio Grande" covered a passel of ground, but she had no doubt this cowboy would have no trouble hanging on to the title. Heck, she'd give him the sexiest-smile-*ever* title. She'd certainly never seen one that made her tummy flutter more.

She moved to the beat of the music with him, the noise of the honky-tonk throbbing around her, the thrill of sexual awareness thrumming through her. With his broad shoulders, lean hips and that killer smile, the man sent sparkling bubbles shimmering over her every feminine nerve. A welcome diversion from the panic that had chased her into the bar in the first place.

He held his hand up, her fingers entwined in his, and twirled her from him.

She spun away until she hit the end of their extended arms, the sound of bass guitars vibrating beneath her feet, the twang of the steel guitar singing in her ears.

He tugged her back, his cowboy hat tipped low, his big silver buckle glinting in the dim light.

She danced back into his arms, his look heating her from the inside out, the sadness lurking in the back of his eyes touching a chord deep within her. They'd sat at the bar for half an hour before they'd wandered out to dance. During that time they'd talked about the Texas heat, the music and a dozen other generic subjects. Now she wanted to know about him.

She flicked one of the pearl snaps on his shirt. "So tell me, cowboy, do these fancy Western clothes mean you're the real deal? Or are they just your let's-go-dancing-and-impress-the-girls duds?"

One corner of his smile hitched wryly. "I'm the real deal, darlin'."

"An honest-to-goodness cowboy, huh?"

"Honest-to-goodness."

Considering her current predicament, she didn't know if that was good or bad. But she wasn't surprised by the answer. He had calluses on his hands, his skin was deeply tanned and his muscles didn't look as though they'd been built in a gym. He looked as if he spent his days under the hot Texas sun wrestling cows and sitting in the saddle. She leaned in close again, enjoying the feel of that work-hardened body. "Do you work nearby?"

"Nope."

"Live nearby?"

"Nope.

She chuckled. "Do you have a thing about talking about yourself? Or are you just short on words?"

He shrugged through the next step. "I might spend my days pushing cattle, but that doesn't mean I share their IQ. I get a pretty filly on my arm, the last thing I'm gonna do is bore her with talk about me. Tell me something about you."

There was more here than a cowboy not wanting to bore a lady. It seemed clear he didn't want to talk about himself. She studied him for a moment, debating whether or not to push. The shadows in his eyes convinced her to let it be. Getting personal might make him think about things he'd rather not. Things he'd possibly come to this bar to forget. Something she understood. "So what do you want to know?"

He thought for a moment, his expression turning playful. "Tell me your three most favorite things in the world?"

That was easy. Chasing fresh powder with her three best friends, Crissy, Mattie and Nell. The nights they stayed up together solving the world's problems—and sometimes their own. The fund-raisers she and those girls put on as the Alpine Angels, helping people with big medical problems and no medical insurance.

But she couldn't say that. Because right now, she feared all that was about to disappear. A fresh wave of panic washed through her, but she pushed it away. She'd come into this bar to forget, too. And with electricity crackling between her and the cowboy like heat lightning gone wild, there were certainly more appealing things to think about. "Let's see, my three favorite things are… Old cars. Good movies. And…" She shot him an impish grin. "Dancing with handsome cowboys."

He shook his head, chuckling. "Forget the stroke-the-cowboy's-ego thing, let's talk about those cars. What kind of old cars do you like?"

So he liked old cars. She smiled. "Well, you have to appreciate the old and grand. The Deusenbergs, Cords and Auburns. And the obscure. The Tuckers and the Bugattis. But the more acquirable are nice, too. You gotta love a '59 Caddy."

"Convertible or hardtop?"

Her smile got a little wider. This was a man who obviously had a preference. "Convertible. Absolutely."

He laughed, the sadness in his eyes almost disappearing as he looked down at her. "The only way to go. Wind in your hair, leather under your butt, highway flying by and nothing but pure style wrapped around you. Beauty, speed and freedom."

Yes. That's just how she imagined she'd feel flying

down the highway in her dream Cadillac. But she had to laugh. "Shouldn't you be describing your horse?"

He shook his head. "My horse has his place. On the range with the sun coming up and a herd of cows stretching toward the horizon he's the best tool, a soothing mode of transportation—and a good friend, too. But when it comes to the perfect ride and good times, the Caddy's damned hard to beat."

Didn't she know it. But the fact that *he* knew it was even better.

"So what color is this Caddy?" His eyes twinkled as he led her around the dance floor. "Pink, I suppose."

"Is there any other color?"

"If there's a pretty blonde at the wheel, I think pink's a prerequisite. Then again, if your handsome cowboy is driving, fire-engine red with ivory interior comes to mind." He spun her away again, then gave her a gentle tug back.

The world sparkled as she twirled back into his arms. "Okay, I might concede that, it's a bit pimpy, but—"

"*Pimpy.* Bite your tongue, woman. The word is *flashy*—with a touch of class."

She laughed. "Maybe. But let's face it, in my fantasies, the blonde's driving, so pink it is."

He shook his head, smiling. "Okay, the blonde's driving. What movie is she going to?"

"Something with lots of action and manly heroes." She waggled a brow. *"The Terminator. The Wind Talkers. X-Men."*

"Thumbs-up to the metal man and Native Americans, but how manly can a hero named Wolverine be?" Devilry sparkled in his eyes.

He was teasing her. And she loved it. It made her feel warm and alive and…wanted. Something she hadn't felt much of lately.

He led her through the other dancing couples, his thighs brushing hers, his arms keeping her close. "How does Miss Cadillac feel about epics? Only the ones with manly heroes, of course."

"Hey, *Lord of the Rings, Braveheart,* I'm there."

He settled his hands at her hips, moving them in seductive cadence with his own.

Man, he felt good. All hard muscle and male heat.

He cocked his head to the side, watching her, his expression as hot as the surface of the sun. "So epics are in. How does she feel about drive-ins?"

Her pulse jumped into overdrive. "Drive-ins? Now those are hard to find these days. But when one's around and the night is hot, parking in the back with the top down and the right man has a certain appeal."

That sexy grin flashed again. "Just the answer I'd expect from a lady driving a pink Caddy." And the glint in his eyes said it was exactly the answer he'd wanted. Rocking her hips with his, he peered at her from beneath the brim of his tan, well-worn cowboy hat.

Desire and need and something less definable—but more powerful—slid through her. Since the moment she'd walked into the bar and their gazes had met, she'd been captivated. Whether by his smile or those sad eyes she couldn't say, but she'd never felt so connected to a man before. She'd certainly never felt such heat.

She ran her hands down his arms, savoring the hardness of muscle, the sharp contrast between male and female. She couldn't believe the energy that surged between them. It was so strong it felt as if there was something cosmic at work. The universe bringing soul mates together.

Yeah, right. Cosmic intervention only happened in fairy tales. And her life had never been a fairy tale. But that didn't mean *something* wasn't happening here. Something more than alcohol and hormones.

She probed a little deeper. "So tell me, what is a handsome cowboy like you doing alone in a crowded honky-tonk on Saturday night?"

He ran a finger down her arm. "I'm not alone."

"You were alone when I walked in."

He looked away from her, his gaze skating over her head to a place much bleaker than the honky-tonk they were in now. "Being alone has its place sometimes."

She studied his face, the grim turn of his lips, the shadows in his eyes. "Maybe. But that doesn't mean it's fun."

"No." His lips twisted wryly. "More often than not it's damned lonely."

Poor cowboy. She knew all about the cold, hollow grip of loneliness. She'd grown up steeped in it. Was afraid it was once again about to invade her life. Is that the pull she felt between them? The instinctive recognition of kindred souls?

Maybe. Maybe not. All she knew was that she couldn't stand the sadness in his eyes. She stretched up on her toes and kissed him, her lips brushing over his.

It was a simple kiss, a comforting kiss.

He drank it in and initiated one of his own.

But there wasn't anything simple about his kiss. The sexual energy that had been smoldering between them caught fire and took off like a brush fire in a windstorm.

She opened her mouth beneath his. He tasted like Jack Daniels and hot male.

Intoxicating.

Tantalizing.

She leaned into him. She wanted to feel him. All of him. He pulled her closer, the hard planes of his body molding to her softer ones, his tongue stroking hers.

The cold wall of loneliness that was sneaking into the periphery of her own life warmed, heated…disappeared. She savored the feel of him against her, the amazing buzz that hummed between them.

He pulled his lips from hers and stared down at her, his eyes dilated, his breathing short and hard. His gaze flicked to the right.

She followed it.

A wide staircase led up to a second level, no doubt to a bank of rentable rooms. Heat poured through her. She knew what he was thinking. Knew he was wondering if they should go up those stairs together.

Should they?

She'd rushed into men's beds before and been hurt. Left alone. She stared up at the cowboy, at the shaggy dark brown hair that peeked out from beneath his hat, at his sad eyes and sexy smile. She felt the connection humming between them, a connection that seemed to go so much deeper than sexual attraction. She knew it was silly to believe the universe had brought her here to meet this man. And yet, it felt that way.

She took hold of her hopelessly romantic heart and tried to make herself think logically, realistically. The universe was *not* an active being, it did *not* bring people together. But…

That didn't mean she hadn't stumbled upon Mr. Right purely by accident. And if that were the case, did she want to throw this night away?

Lordy, why didn't life come with a road map? Or a crystal ball? Was that too much to ask? She didn't need a giant atlas that would show her every tiny road she might wander down, or a crystal ball that would tell her every second of her future. Just…*something* to get her through to tomorrow morning.

But all she had to guide her was her heart.

She'd felt lonely when she'd walked into this bar. His sexy smile and easy banter had eased that ache. And his kiss had melted it away completely. She wanted to hang on to that warmth. And she wanted to chase his loneliness away, too.

She looked back to find his gaze still on her. She ran

a finger down his jaw, savoring the purely male rough-
ness of his five-o'clock shadow, the deep warmth of his
skin. "We could burn this hotel down around us."

"We could burn this town down around us. But
should we?"

"I know about loneliness, too, cowboy. Know how
deep it can sink into your bones. I don't want to be alone
tonight. Let's see what else we have in common besides
a love of old cars and good movies."

He shouldn't take her up on her invitation. He absolutely shouldn't. He'd come to this bar, gotten the same
room he got every year so the bartender would have a
place to dump him once he was unconscious, and then
he'd headed to the bar to drink himself into oblivion.

And he'd been well on his way to that blissful unconscious state when he'd looked up and seen a gray-
eyed angel staring at him from across the noisy,
smokey bar. Angel?

Hardly the word that had popped into his brain when
he'd first seen her. The woman had exuded sex. With
her sultry gray eyes, bee-stung lips and lush curves
she'd obviously been made for sin. Hot, steamy, sheet-
twisting sin.

And since sheet-twisting sin was his favorite remedy for chasing away the bleak emptiness that had en-
tered his life four years ago, he'd gotten to his feet and
sauntered over to the barstool next to her.

But after five minutes of conversation, he'd discovered an openness about her, a guilelessness, a...whole-someness that had no doubt put the angel image in his head. And should have had him walking away. Then and now. Using an angel to hide from the cold barrenness of his life would undoubtedly get him a few extra years in hell.

But he couldn't walk away. Not tonight. Her wholesomeness combined with her overt sexuality was like a warm, thawing breeze. A breeze he wanted to feel more of. Needed to feel more of.

He brushed his lips over hers. "Upstairs sounds good." Before she changed her mind, before *he* changed his mind, he pulled her up the stairs. He hit the top landing and made his way to his room where he took his room card from his pocket and swiped it through the lock.

A red light blinked.

Damn. He stared down at the card, trying to make sense of the arrows and instructions printed on the back, but the alcohol was fuzzing his brain. He swiped the card again.

Another red light.

The fates trying to make him reconsider?

Maybe. But he wasn't changing his mind. Life bubbled from her like pure, clean water from a spring. He needed to feel that tonight. Needed to taste it.

He swiped the card again. A green light shone back at him. He pushed the handle down before the damned thing changed its mind, and then he started to pull the wholesome love goddess into the room behind him.

But her feet didn't move.

He looked back to her, praying she hadn't changed her mind.

She stared at him with those gorgeous gray eyes. "I don't know your name."

"Tom. My name's Tom."

An easy smile turned her lips. "So what are we waiting for, Tom?"

Not a damned thing. He pulled her into the room and into his arms. He had his mouth on hers before the door closed, heat and need stampeding through him.

She tasted like sweet wine, raw sex and American-pie goodness. A lethal combination. He deepened the kiss, trying to pull her very essence into him. Finally he dragged his lips from hers. His breathing hard and fast, every bit as anxious as the rest of him, he pulled her farther into the room, next to the bed. Taking a few steps back, he took her in.

Her sleeveless, tailored top accented her full breasts. And those low, hip-hugging jeans? Holy Texas night! Had he ever seen such great curves? His fingers itched to touch. But he resisted the urge. He wanted to make every second last. He tipped his head toward the collar of her shirt. "Unbutton your blouse."

With a wicked, playful smile she flipped her long, shiny curtain of straight, blond hair behind her shoulders. Then she unbuttoned the first button, her gaze never leaving his. "What are you hoping for underneath? Lace or white cotton?"

Naked skin. But she was having too much fun teasing him and he was having too much fun being teased not to play along. "Lace. Who can resist a woman who wears lace?" And he couldn't picture any woman who drove a '59 pink Cadillac wearing anything but.

Her smile turned a little more wicked. "Yeah? Well, we'll just have to see, won't we?" She worked the next button—slowly—uncovering another patch of tan, silky skin.

His mouth went dry and he sent a prayer heavenward, resisting the urge to help her with those buttons. But it would purely be a shame to hurry this night. He stuck his hands into his pockets and watched her fingers work the next button free.

The flash of nail polish caught his attention. Not bright red like one would expect on a sinning siren, but a light, pretty pink. Like one would expect on a woman with a gentle nature and a sweet heart. He swallowed hard, another wave of desire pounding through him.

Her fingers hesitated on the next button, that sultry gaze meeting his. "Am I in this alone?"

Alone. The word echoed in his head. He'd dragged her up here because he couldn't stand the solitariness of his own life. "Hell, no." He jerked the tail of his shirt out of his pants, grabbed the plackets and pulled. With a rapid pop, pop, pop, the pearl snaps gave way. He sloughed the shirt off and tossed it aside.

She chuckled, low and sexy. "That's what I like, a team player." Her gaze skated over his bare chest. "Very nice, cowboy. Get all that muscle wrestling cows?"

Her open admiration sent another wave of heat slamming through him. "Some of it." He tipped his head toward her stalled fingers. "Planning on catching up with me anytime soon?"

The corners of her mouth tipped up mischievously and the next button popped open, exposing a hint of mouthwatering cleavage and a narrow bit of peach lace.

Peach lace. An innocent color to contrast with the sheer, erotic material. He wanted to groan out loud.

She popped the next button…and the next…and *finally* the last.

He stared, anticipation pouring through him.

With an easy flip of her wrists, she flicked the shirt open, displaying the delicate line of her rib cage, the tiny curve of her waist—and the most gorgeous, perfect breasts he'd ever seen.

Great thundering hooves. His palms broke out in a cold sweat. He moved closer, the toes of his boots nipping the toes of her tennies. He swiped his hat off and sent it spinning to a nearby chair—he didn't want anything impeding his view. Including her blouse. He flicked the collar. "Why don't you toss this pretty little thing over with mine."

She shrugged off the shirt, gave it a toss and peeked up at him through long, sooty lashes. "Now what do you have in mind?" Her voice was low, husky, inviting. Her pose—shoulders back, breasts forward—pure dare.

He wanted to laugh out loud. This filly was a handful. Any man who intended to roam the range with her would have to run hard to keep up. But he only had to worry about keeping up tonight. Not a problem. "Darlin', it's not about what's in my mind." He cupped the peach-covered globes, her heat branding his palms.

There was nothing fake about these babies. They were all hers. Full and soft, and Lordy he wanted to taste them. He dipped his head and trailed kisses along the top of the lace, his tongue sneaking out to taste the hot, soft flesh, his hands kneading the full, pliant mounds. The fit of his jeans became downright painful.

She grabbed his shoulders, a soft hiss falling from her lips, her nipples peaking against his palms.

Beautiful…and responsive. He drew in her scent. Something sweet and tangy that came out of a bottle. And something warm and alluring that was the woman herself. He took another deep breath, savoring the erotic combination as he moved his mouth down to the good part and drew her nipple in, lace and all.

Her fingers bit into his shoulders and her hips rocked forward, a needy sigh floating over his head.

He canted his own hips forward, stroking hers, but the double layer of denim didn't allow him anywhere near the intimacy he craved. He suckled hard one more time and pulled his lips from her. "There are entirely too many clothes here."

"I'll second that motion."

There was a flurry of activity as they both discarded shoes and pants. He beat her by a hair and stood back and watched as she finished kicking her jeans off. Now she wore nothing but her lacy bra and matching panties. She looked like candy from the gods. His breath caught, and his sex flexed. Had he ever seen anything so beautiful?

Or mind-numbingly sexy?

He blinked and she was in his arms, her warm body pressed against his as she nipped playfully at his lips. "Kiss me, cowboy."

He slid his hand behind her neck, the silky strands of her hair teasing his fingers, and pulled her lips to his.

Warm.

Heady.

Impossibly sweet.

He deepened the kiss, savoring her.

She shivered, a greedy moan vibrating in her throat, her body stroking his.

Desire shot through him, white-hot and lightning-quick. Enough playing around. In one quick move, he lifted her, tossed her in the middle of the bed, then divested her of those cute little panties and settled between her legs.

She laughed up at him, her tantalizing heat snuggled up tight against his aching need, her eyes sparkling with delight, darkening with desire. "Why do I get the impression you've tossed more than a few poor calves in just that manner?"

He smiled back. "A cowboy's gotta do what a cowboy's gotta do." And right now he needed to be in her. Needed to feel her wet heat wrapped around him. Needed to feel the communion of one human being connected to another.

He nudged her thighs farther apart with his knees and nestled down—stopping just short of the gates to heaven, a soft curse echoing through his head. "Protection. We need protection."

Realization flickered in her eyes. She groaned in frustration. "I have one in my purse. But I left it downstairs."

"Don't worry, I know the bartender, he'll realize it's sitting there unattended and tuck it away safely. And I have protection, but it's in my jeans—*way* over there."

She chuckled, low and sultry. "Well, hurry up then."

It didn't take him long to make his way to his jeans and extract his wallet. He fished for the ever-ready condom inside it, opened it and started rolling it on.

She watched him with unabashed admiration. "Faster, cowboy."

Fresh need surged through him. He made quick work of the task at hand and joined her on the bed, the ache in his groin driving him harder than a roweled spur drove a bull. And then he was sinking into her.

Hot and wet and leather-glove tight.

He gritted his teeth, holding on to his control by the barest of threads. Heaven couldn't be so sweet.

A soft sigh escaped her lips. She looked up at him,

her gray eyes dove-soft as she pushed a lock of fallen hair out of his eyes. "Do you believe in fate, cowboy? In the gods bringing two people together?"

He believed a man made his own fate—or screwed it up. And in his experience the gods were a fickle, twisted bunch. But there was something in her expression—a wishfulness, a hopefulness—that told him that wasn't the answer she wanted.

And he couldn't stand the thought of saying anything that would turn her open trusting expression into one of disappointment and scorn. Or have her walking out. He tipped his shoulder philosophically. "We're here, aren't we?"

A slow, joyful smile curved her lips. "Yes we are." She rocked gently beneath him, taking him deeper.

Fire roared through him.

She stared up at him with those pretty gray eyes. Something sweet and warm wound its way through him. Tomorrow would be soon enough to go back to his empty existence.

He took hold of her wrists and held her hands above her head. "Hold on, darlin', it's going to be a wild ride."

Chapter Two

Air-conditioning blasting, Josie drove down the bumpy, gravel road leading onto the Big T. Her car hit a giant pothole, bottoming out with a loud crunch, but she didn't care.

She'd woken up alone this morning.

Heart-crushingly alone.

After the most incredible night she'd ever had.

She dropped her head back against the car seat. What was it with her that she couldn't get this guy thing right? She liked men. Loved men. Loved their big, hard bodies. The way they moved. The way they talked. The way they smelled. So why couldn't she find one that wouldn't leave her?

She'd been positive last night that there'd been a real connection between her and the handsome cowboy. Something that might have a future. But he'd fooled her. Darling Tom had been nothing more than a tomcat looking for a good time. And she'd walked right into his arms, eyes wide-open—if a little clouded by her own foolish hopes.

She sighed, shaking her head. When would she get it right?

Not today apparently. She stared at the approaching low-lying hills that ringed the Big T ranch. Crissy's new home. No reprieve from her dark mood there. She'd pulled off the highway into the bar last night because she wasn't ready to face what awaited her at the Big T. Because she wasn't ready to face her friend and fellow Alpine Angel, Crissy Albreit.

Correction. Crissy McCade. Crissy was married now, to the foreman of the Big T, the ranch Crissy had inherited six months ago. A ranch profitable enough that if Crissy chose, she could easily fund the Alpine Angels' charity from the Big T's annual income.

Josie's stomach clenched. She feared that with her new husband and new home, Crissy wouldn't need the Alpine Angels anymore.

And the Angels were the only family Josie had ever had.

She drew a long breath, trying to steady her nerves. How many times had she begun to settle into a family as a kid, begun to feel like she belonged, only to have the family decide they were better off without her and send her on to the next foster home?

Too many times to count.

And she was afraid it was about to happen again.

She took another deep breath. Using the Big T for the next fund-raiser was a perfectly logical idea. Crissy owned the Big T. They wouldn't have to pay anyone to use it or get any special permits to have the event. And the Big T had just about everything they needed to put on the rodeo: the corrals, the arena, most of the livestock. Very little money would have to be spent for preparation. It made absolute sense to put on a rodeo instead of holding one of their usual alpine events. It didn't mean Crissy was trying to phase out her friends.

But it might, an insidious little voice whispered in the back of her head. You know how it happens. People's lives change. They move on, leaving old friends and old acquaintances behind.

Josie closed her eyes, willing the words and her insecurity away, doing her best to hang on to reason. Even if every event Crissy put on from now on was some type of cowboy event, it wouldn't necessarily mean she was leaving the Angels behind. The worst it could mean was that to keep her place in the group Josie would have to develop rodeo skills the way she'd developed snowboarding skills over the years. She could do that. She was athletic. And Crissy had a ranch full of cowboys who could teach Josie everything she needed to know.

Handsome cowboys. Cowboys who would make her forget all about that rat Tom.

Yeah.

Plan of action in mind, she drove around the bank of low-lying hills, the heretofore empty Texas countryside exploding into civilization and activity. The large valley held several buildings. Houses, barns and a long two-story bunkhouse situated in the middle of a sea of corrals. Cows and horses filled the metal pens, their moos and neighs filling the air. Cowboys by the dozen milled around, taking care of the big animals and doing other chores.

The Big T—in all its chaotic glory.

She sighed. Ready or not, here she was. She followed the wide gravel road through the busy corrals toward the big house Crissy's father, Warner Trevarrow, had lived in before he'd passed away. She pulled up in front of the huge, fancy log home with its floor-to-ceiling windows and wraparound porches. It was where she'd be staying while she was here. She put the car in Park and got out, the Texas heat hitting her like a brick wall.

She turned to look over at the small house on the other side of the dirt road. It was the Big T's original homestead—and where Crissy now lived with her new husband, Tate. But it didn't look like anyone was home. There were no vehicles parked out front and no one appeared to be moving around inside.

Behind her, the door to the big house opened, and

the sound of cowboy boots rang on the wooden porch. "Hey, Josie. See you finally made it."

She peeked over her shoulder to find Braxton standing on the porch. The handsome cowboy with his broad shoulders, narrow hips and whipcord-lean body was Crissy's bookkeeper and financial advisor. Josie had met him only a few times. She liked him. There was a profound quietness about him, an inner peace, a self-confidence that made him easy to be around. Which was a good thing because the ranch office where he worked was in the big house. She'd be running into him quite a bit.

She nodded. "Yep, finally here. I got…a bit delayed yesterday."

He tipped his head toward the old homestead. "Looking for Crissy?"

Doing her best to bury her bleak mood, she forced a smile to her lips. "She around?"

"In the barn with Tate. Why don't you wander on over, let her know you're here. I can take your bags up to the room you usually use."

She opened her back door, giving him access to her bags. "Thanks, Brax."

He strode out to her car, his gaze sliding over her, zeroing in on her face. "You okay?"

She never had been good at hiding her feelings. But she forced the corners of her lips up another notch. "I'm fine. Just a little tired. It was a long drive." With a quick wave, she strode away before he could ask more questions.

She made her way through the corrals toward the big red barn. The huge sliding doors at the end were open in deference to the heat. She walked in, the smell of hay and horses filling her nose even as the cooler temperature of the covered space gave her a bit of relief from the Texas sun.

She heard human murmuring and the rustle of straw several stalls down. Crissy was probably in playing with one of the horses. Josie wandered down the wide, cement aisle, the voice getting louder and more distinct as she got farther into the barn. Correction, voic*es*, one of which was definitely Crissy's. The other, lower, masculine one was Tate's.

"*Ouch.*" Crissy's high-pitched squeal echoed through the barn followed by the sound of someone scurrying through straw. And then, "That little devil just bit me in the *butt.*"

Tate laughed, a low, intimate sound. The kind of laugh only a mate would use. "You gotta give the boy points for knowing the good parts."

Josie smiled, a dull ache throbbing in her chest. There was so much intimacy in Tate's teasing—so much love.

She finally found the stalls the voices were coming from. But Crissy and Tate hadn't noticed her yet, so Josie stood quietly, watching the action.

Crissy was in a stall with little Moe, a horse Crissy had helped deliver several months ago. The spindly foal had done some growing since Josie's last trip to the

Big T. His head reached Crissy's shoulder now and he was standing in a corner of the stall, mischief sparkling in his big brown equine eyes as he stared at Crissy.

Crissy stood a few feet from him in the middle of the straw-filled enclosure, rubbing her backside and scowling at her husband. "It's not funny. That hurt."

Tate was in the next stall over with a big, brown horse he'd obviously been brushing. But he'd abandoned the task to lean on the wall separating the box-like spaces, one hand—the hand holding the brush—dangling between the bars separating the top of the two stalls. With his cowboy hat tipped low, his pearly whites gleaming in the barn's dim light, he smiled at his wife. "I'll bet it hurt. His teeth aren't so small anymore, are they? Which is why when he was little and he'd nip you, I told you to get after him. But no, you said he was too cute."

Crissy's scowl deepened. "I hate men who say I told you so."

Tate shook his head. "No, you don't. At least not this one. You love me." His look turned downright seductive. "And if it still stings, we could get out of here, go inside. I could kiss it better."

Definite interest flashed in Crissy's expression at Tate's suggestion. But she didn't give in. She tipped her head up and looked down her nose at him. "You'd like that, wouldn't you?"

He chuckled again, that low sexy laugh. "Absolutely. And so would you."

Josie's chest tightened. Would a man ever look at her the way Tate was looking at Crissy? With all that desire and love just oozing from his pores?

Crissy held on to her pique for, oh, another half second. And then she crumbled. "Maybe I would." She strode toward the separating wall, her look turning as amorous as his.

Josie didn't know what they thought they were going to do through the bars of the stall, but she wasn't going to wait to find out. She cleared her throat. "Hey, guys."

Crissy's head swung in her direction, her expression brightening as she spotted Josie standing in the aisle. "Hey, where have you been? I thought you were coming in last night."

"I got a little delayed." But that was the last thing she wanted to think about. Or talk about.

"Why didn't you call?"

"Because I'm over twenty-one, mama hen."

"Which just means you can drink," Tate said from his stall, his tone serious, admonishing. "It doesn't exempt you from traffic accidents and other disasters. We were worried when you didn't show up."

She wanted to believe they'd thought about her, worried about her. "Sorry, next time I'll pick up the phone. So what are you doing to poor Moe? Torturing him?"

Crissy rolled her eyes, shaking her head. "I'm trying to teach the little beast to hold his feet up for the farrier. But it's not going very well. He just bit me."

Josie smiled. "So I heard."

A tinge of pink colored Crissy's cheeks. "Yeah, what else did you hear?"

She looked to Tate, smiling. "Enough to know hubby maybe wouldn't mind taking a little nip of his own."

"Okay, I'm outta here." Red crawling up his neck, Tate pulled his hand from the bars and left the stall, carrying the brush. As he stepped into the lighter area of the aisle, he gave Josie a good once-over. His gaze settled on her face. "You okay?"

Man, she must be the most open book in the world. She waved away his concern just as she had Braxton's and forced some levity into her voice. "I'm fine. It was just a long drive."

He hesitated, as if deciding whether or not to believe her. But then he gave his head a single nod and headed down the aisle toward the open door.

"Hey." Crissy stuck her head out of the stall and hollered at her disappearing husband. "Send Buckle-boy to the house, will you? I want him to meet Josie and set up lessons with her for tomorrow."

Tate shook his head, his steps never faltering. "I'll tell him, but with that summons you'll be lucky if he shows up by sundown." He disappeared out the door.

Josie looked back to Crissy, raising a brow in question.

Crissy smiled, disappearing into the stall. "Buckle-boy's not real fond of the nickname." She slipped the halter from Moe's head and left the stall. She gave Josie a big, welcoming hug, then leaned back far enough to see Josie's face. "Okay, what's wrong?"

Josie always talked with Crissy when her love life went astray. But she wasn't ready to talk about last night. Not yet. She shook her head, stepping back. "Nothing. Like I said, it was a long drive. And what kind of nickname is Buckle-boy, anyway?"

Crissy made a face, hanging Moe's halter on the front of his stall. "A fitting one. But we're not talking about him. We're talking about you. And drop the long drive bit. I know that look. This is about a man, isn't it?"

Josie plowed her fingers through her hair. "Maybe."

Crissy snorted. "Don't maybe me. I know you, and— Oh God, that's why you didn't show up last night. You were with a man, weren't you?" Her expression turn empathetic. "And he hurt you."

Josie sighed. She ought to know hiding things from Crissy was impossible. "Yeah, I was and he did. But it was my own damned fault. *And* I don't want to talk about it."

"You never do. But you always feel better after you have. Come on, we can talk about the rodeo on the way to the house. But once we're there, you're dishing." She linked her arm with Josie's and started down the aisle. "So, are you ready to learn how to ride a bronc?"

No, she wasn't. In fact, having her butt tossed onto hard dirt held damned little appeal. She already felt bruised enough. And thinking about the rodeo just sent that panicky feeling racing up her spine again. Which she tried desperately to ignore. But couldn't. "Tell me again why we're having a rodeo for this fund-raiser instead of swishing down a mountain?"

Surprise creased Crissy's brow as they walked into the hot Texas sun. "You don't like the idea of a rodeo?"

"I didn't say that." She didn't know if she liked the idea or not. She only knew it scared her. "It's just that we made our name snowboarding."

"Yeah, but we've occasionally done other sports for fund-raisers. Case in point, swimming with sharks last spring, remember?"

"I remember. And it was fun. But especially because that event wasn't our usual alpine one makes me think this one should have been on a mountain."

Crissy looked away, something suspiciously close to guilt crossing her face.

Unease shimmered through Josie. And when her friend said nothing for the next few steps, she pushed. "Crissy?"

Crissy took a few more silent steps, then looked back, her expression sheepish. "It's just that I like it here on the ranch. And there are so many reasons to have the events here. We've talked about them. The fact that rodeo is an up-and-coming sport. I already have the four corporations we need lined up for the big bucks. And the location is good. Great actually. It's going to be easier for the public to get here to pledge their money. *And,* because so many cowboys in the area rodeo, we're going to have more contestants for the corporations to pay up on. And, of course, the cowboys competing are donating their entry fees and winnings to the cause, as well. This is going to be the biggest event the Angels have ever put on."

And with all the cowboys, why would she need the Angels? "Does that mean we're never going back to the mountains?"

"We could still go back," Crissy hedged. "If the rodeo doesn't work out. But I think it's going to."

Josie's worst fears were coming to fruition. If she didn't adapt to this new sport, her connection to the Angels would disappear. And the thought of losing that connection...

She didn't want to think about it. Couldn't think about it. Not until she knew for sure how things would pan out. So she forced her mind on to happier thoughts. "So when are the other girls coming?"

"Unfortunately, Nell and Mattie won't be along until just before the rodeo."

"That won't give them much practice time."

"I know, but their bosses absolutely refuse to let them off earlier. Luckily, they've both found someone in their areas to work with, so they won't be arriving totally unprepared. And with the other cowboys pitching in, we'll be okay even if the four of us don't rake in the bucks like we usually do."

With the other cowboys pitching in.

She squelched the dread that phrase brought.

Crissy stopped at her car. "Do you have bags to bring in?"

She shook her head. "Brax took them up to my room."

"Good. Let's get out of this heat."

She followed Crissy into the house. The air-conditioning was a welcome relief as she took a quick glance around. Nothing had changed from her last visit. The round stone fireplace still stood in the middle of the enormous, open room, offering a central gathering place. Sunshine poured in through the floor-to-ceiling windows that lined the front wall. The high ceiling soared overhead.

"Let's go into Dad's office," Crissy said, striding by the gatherings of furniture that provided conversation areas here and there. "We're less likely to be disturbed there."

Since the Big T's offices were located off the sunny room, it wasn't unusual for a cowboy who needed something to wander in. The solitude of the back office sounded good. They walked by the staircase that led to the upstairs bedrooms to the office doors on the back wall. Crissy pushed open the one on the right and strode in, Josie on her heels.

As expected, nothing had changed here, either. Since Crissy had never known her father while he was alive because of an ugly misunderstanding between her parents, Josie imagined she wanted to surround herself with what little she had of him now. And this room exuded the personality of Warner Trevarrow. From the leather-bound books lining the walls, to the elk's head hanging above the big mahogany desk, to the picture of Warner with two-year-old Crissy sitting on a pretty white pony prominently displayed on the desk's corner.

Another twinge of envy squeezed Josie. Despite the fact Crissy had discovered her father's love only after his death, she'd still had it. And she was reminded of it every day as she worked on the ranch Warner had built for his missing daughter.

What would it be like to have had a father who loved her? A family who loved her?

Wasted emotions. Josie would never know. She pushed the thoughts away and dropped into a leather chair on the visitor's side of the desk while Crissy dropped into the big wingback chair on the other side.

As soon as Crissy's backside hit the scarred leather she locked her gaze on Josie. "Okay, what happened last night?"

Josie dropped her head back against the chair and stared at the ceiling. "Crissy…"

"I'm not letting you off the hook here, girl, so cough it up."

Josie sighed. Crissy was like a terrier when something was bothering one of them. She'd pick and push until they gave in and spilled their guts. And afterward, they usually did feel better. "I don't even know where to start."

"How about where you met this guy. *When* you met him? I talked to you a week ago and there was no mention of him."

She briefly thought about ducking and running, but even on a spread the size of the Big T, sooner or later Crissy would hunt her down. "That's because I didn't know him then. I met him last night."

"You met him *last night?*"

She nodded dismally. "I was on my way here and… And I thought a drink might relax me. I'd been driving all day and my shoulders were tight, sore." Not exactly the truth, but close enough. "Anyway, I stopped at this bar along the highway. And… I met this guy."

"You went to bed with a guy you met in a bar? A *highway* bar! A guy you knew *how long?*"

Josie winced, heat suffusing her cheeks. "How do you know I went to bed with him?"

"Because you were supposed to get here last night and you didn't get here until this morning."

"Okay, so I'd only known him about an hour. But—"

"But *what? Josie,* what were you thinking?"

Frustration at the perfidious Tom and her own gullibility pounded through her. "I don't know. I just… We just…clicked. It seemed so…*right*." But it had obviously been so, so wrong.

"Josie, the man could have been a serial killer. Even for you, Miss Gotta-have-a-guy-in-my-life, this was crazy."

She slumped back into her chair. "I know. It's just… He was so sweet and sad and sexy and he liked old cars and…" And he took the loneliness away.

Now Crissy groaned and dropped her head onto the desk with an audible thunk. "Josie, Josie, Josie. What are we going to do with you?" Her words echoed off the mahogany surface.

Josie looked at her friend all but banging her head on the desk, and from somewhere deep inside her, a laugh bubbled up. She shook her head. "God, I am such an idiot."

Crissy picked up her head, chuckling with her. "Not an idiot. Just…a hopeless romantic."

Josie shot her a droll look.

"All right, maybe a little bit of an idiot."

Josie shook her head and rubbed at her eyes. "What is wrong with me? Why can't I get this guy thing right?"

"I don't know. Maybe you're trying too hard. Maybe you don't have enough faith in yourself. Sometimes I think you go to bed with the guys you meet because you don't think they'll stay around otherwise."

Her stomach sank. "Maybe they won't."

Crissy splayed her hands. "Then why on earth would you want them around?"

"Because…" The answer lodged in her throat.

"Because *what?*"

"Because I keep hoping if they stay around long enough, they'll fall in love with me." The words were out before she could stop them.

Crissy raised a sardonic brow. "And how's that working for you?"

"Well, obviously not real well, Dr. Phil. But—"

"No buts. Come on, Josie, have a little faith in yourself. You have so much more to offer these guys than your body. Give them a little time to find that out before you give the store away."

She thought of the men that had come and gone in her past. There'd been more than a few. None of them had stayed longer than a couple months. Giving the store away clearly hadn't worked. Maybe a new strategy was in order. "Okay, my days as a hopeless romantic are over. From now on, any man in my life is going to have to prove himself before he gets an invitation into my bed."

"Good for you."

A knock sounded on the door.

Crissy shifted her gaze to the oak panel. "Ah, this should be Buckle-boy. Your teacher for the next month. Come on in," she hollered.

The door swung open behind her. Cowboy boots rang on the wooden floor.

Crissy waved a hand toward Josie. "Tommy Ray, I'd like you to meet Josie. The first Angel to arrive on the scene for your invaluable tutelage. Josie, the Big T's rodeo champ, Tommy Ray."

Josie turned in her chair and stared into the saddest eyes she'd ever seen, and the sexiest smile this side of the Rio Grande.

Chapter Three

Tommy Ray stared at the woman sitting in the chair in front of the big mahogany desk.

The angel from last night.

His body surged, but he took a quick rein on his reaction. Not only had last night been one he had no intention of repeating, but this was apparently not just any angel.

She was one of Crissy's Angels.

He couldn't count how many ways that was a bad thing.

He swallowed hard, forced the smile back to his lips and held his hand out, putting the ball in her court. Whether she wanted to acknowledge knowing him or not would be her decision. After that...

God knew.

She just stared at his hand, a million emotions racing across her face. One of them clearly pain.

Guilt niggled at his conscience. He'd suspected she'd hoped for more than a single night of fun. And he'd snuck out in the early hours of the morning while she'd been sleeping to avoid any complicated scenes. Not very chivalrous. But come on, she was a big girl. She'd picked him up in a bar. She knew how the game was played.

But she didn't look all that big right now. She looked small and vulnerable and hurt.

Damn.

From her seat behind the desk Crissy looked back and forth between the angel and him. Suddenly, a light went on in her eyes. An unhappy light. "Oh God, Josie, don't tell me *this* is the guy from last night." She hooked a thumb toward him.

Josie looked away from them both, her cheeks flushing a guilty hue.

Busted.

Crissy groaned. "Oh, girl."

Josie pushed up from her chair, her lips pressed into a hard, thin line. "I'm outta here. You're going to have to find another cowboy to teach me what I need to know, and teach it to me somewhere he's not." She rushed out of the office, slamming the door behind her.

He didn't know whether to run after her or let her

go. He looked to Crissy, thinking she might know what her friend needed.

She glared at him from behind the desk. "Let me get this straight. You're in a bar with probably fifty other women and you pick *my* girlfriend for one of your nights of debauchery."

"I didn't know she was your girlfriend. And what kind of word is that, *debauchery?* For crying out loud, you make it sound like I'm defiling young innocents. Josie was a willing participant." Damned willing.

"That is not an excuse," Crissy spat, stabbing an angry finger at him. "And not knowing who Josie was isn't an excuse, either."

He shook his head. "I'm not sure a man needs an excuse with that woman. She's more potent than an ocean full of oysters."

Her eyes narrowed, but she didn't say anything.

Not a surprise. She was no doubt used to men chasing Josie—in droves.

She pushed up from her chair and paced away from the desk, obviously trying to get a hold of her temper. When she turned back, her eyes were narrow blue bands of warning. "I like you, Tommy Ray. Despite the stupidity you display in your personal life, I like you. I always have. You work well with the other cowboys. You work hard. You take care of your mom and dad and help with your brothers and sisters. *But*…you hurt my girl again, I'll carve your heart out and feed it to the nearest cur, got it?"

She was coming in loud and clear. "Got it."

"Good. Now hear this. One month from today we're putting on a rodeo. I expect Josie to be there. I expect her to be ready. If you don't know someone else as talented as you, someone else who can get her as ready as you can, you've got some fast-talking to do. And some big-time apologizing." She cocked her head, listening to the sound of footsteps pounding down the stairs outside the office. "My guess is that's Josie now, coming back down after retrieving her bags from her room. Sounds like she's leaving. Best get a move on."

Dammit. He'd screwed up big this time. He strode to the door, jerked it open, stepped out and pulled it closed behind him. He didn't have a clue how he was going to save this thing, but he sure as hell didn't want an audience while he tried.

Josie was heading his way, her footsteps long and determined.

He stepped in front of her. "Josie, wait."

She sidestepped him without missing a beat.

Damn. He strode after her, the Texas heat hitting him as they stepped out onto the porch. "Dang it, Josie, hold on. You can't just storm off like this."

"Watch me." She stepped off the porch and headed for her car.

He leaped off the porch, made a quick move to get to her car before she did and leaned against the door. The hot metal seared his ass through his Wranglers, but he didn't budge. He crossed his arms over his chest, letting her know she wasn't going anywhere.

She narrowed those gray eyes on him, but there was no invitation in them now. In fact, murder seemed to be uppermost in her mind. "Get out of my way, cowboy. Before I have to hurt you."

Good, he could handle her anger. The hurt that had been so clear in the office was a little harder to take. "Before anyone goes anywhere we need to talk."

She cocked a single brow. "You made it pretty clear last night, or should I say this morning, that talking wasn't your thing."

He bumped up the brim of his hat with an impatient knuckle. "I didn't think there was anything to say. We'd had a great night, but I didn't see any reason to stick around for an awkward goodbye."

She looked away.

"Look, we both went up those stairs knowing one night was probably all we'd have."

She snapped her gaze back to him, accusation darkening her eyes. "You said you believed in fate. That you believed in the gods bringing two people together."

"What? They can't bring people together for one night?"

She narrowed her eyes on him. "You knew that's not what I meant."

More guilt assailed him. He sighed. "Yeah, I did. But I was *in* you and you obviously wanted me to believe. What the hell did you think I was going to say?"

Her lips trembled, but she managed to keep her chin up. "So it was just a line?"

Hell, yes, it was just a line. He'd have said anything at that moment to keep her under him. He'd been half-drunk and feeling damned sorry for himself—and her wholesome, sweet goddessness had brought him to his knees.

Something she should not suffer for.

He gentled his voice, coaxing. "Come on, you didn't really believe you were going to find Prince Charming in a bar, did you?"

She looked away, pink tinging her cheeks, tears swelling in her eyes.

Well, hell. She had.

He didn't know who was the biggest fool standing here, her or him. He sighed again. It didn't matter who was the biggest fool. He was the one who had to fix it. Not because Crissy had told him to, but because in that one moment of weakness, he'd lied. Led her to believe there might be a tomorrow for them when he knew there wouldn't be any such thing.

He took a deep breath and met her angry, hurting gaze. "I'm sorry. I screwed up. I shouldn't have misled you the way I did. And I apologize for it."

"Fine. Apology accepted. Now get out of my way."

A humorless laugh echoed in his head. Apology accepted? Yeah, right. He ran a hand down his face. "Can't. Not until you put your bags back in your room and we set up a lesson for tomorrow."

"It'll snow pink, right here in your own little baking corner of hell, cowboy, before that happens." She tried to nudge him out of the way with her suitcase.

He spread his feet wider, rooting himself to the ground. "Then you better get your winter coat out for tomorrow morning, darlin'. Because with only a month until the rodeo, you're going to need to get practicing if you want to be ready. Unless, of course, you've decided the charity can make do with one less Angel."

"Don't be ridiculous. I have no intention of letting down the charity or the little girl who's relying on us. But I don't need to work with you for that. Crissy will find me someone else."

"Wrong. She told me to find someone else, providing there was someone else as qualified. But there isn't."

Those gray eyes narrowed. "You cannot possibly be the only cowboy in Texas who knows how to throw a rope or hang on to an angry bull for eight seconds."

"Six. The Professional Women's Rodeo Association only requires a gal hang on to her bull for six seconds. And no, I'm not the only cowboy around who has the skills you need, but I'm the best. And with only a month to get ready, you're going to need the best. Providing, of course, that you intend to make the most money you can."

She stared at him, her hands choking the handles of her bags, her lips pressing into a thin, white line.

After the first five minutes he'd spent with her, he'd

learned enough to know she wasn't the kind of woman who could, in good conscience, give less than her all. Not when a young girl needed the money the Angels could raise to stay alive. He had her.

And she knew it.

She shot him a black scowl. "You play dirty, Tommy Ray."

He gave his head a single nod. "When I have to."

She shook her head, her lips twisted angrily. "Fine. Where and when do I meet you tomorrow?"

A sliver of relief slid through him. No cur would be eating his heart today. "See that small corral next to the barn?" He pointed toward the pen.

"I see it."

"Tomorrow morning, bright and early."

"Fine." She turned on her heel and started back to the house, her curvy hips kicking from side to side with each angry stride.

His fingers burned as he remembered how that heart-shaped bottom had felt snuggled in his palms. He closed his eyes and gritted his teeth. Dallying with the sweet love goddess was out. It didn't matter how sexy she was, how sweet she was. If he hadn't known it before, the pain he'd seen in her eyes this morning had made it abundantly clear Josie Quinn wasn't into meaningless, sexual flings. She was looking for something real.

And he didn't do real.

Not anymore.

* * *

The next morning Josie sat at the small glass-and-wrought-iron table in the kitchen, sipping her coffee. It had been a long sleepless night. She was tired and tense and counting on the caffeine to boost her energy level and steady her nerves. She glanced at the paper in front of her. *Casey's Gazette*, the small local paper. She eyed the bold headline. Carlson Imports New Breed Of Beef.

Great. Cows. Everywhere she looked, cows and more cows. The animals were screwing up her life. Well, she didn't have to start her day reading about them. She skipped to the next article. Find Your Perfect Mate!—New Resident Opens Dating Service.

Oh, good, the other bane of her existence. Men. Giving up on the paper, she sipped her coffee and stared at the earth-tone walls, her mind wandering back to yesterday.

She'd spent a good portion of last evening with Crissy, talking and catching up. It had become obvious early in the gabfest that Josie's fears were warranted. Crissy's new husband and the Big T were definitely taking over Crissy's life. Which, for Crissy, was a good thing.

It meant Crissy's marriage was going well. After growing up poorer than the proverbial church mouse, being bounced from one seedy apartment to the next as she struggled to take care of her sick mother, a mother who'd died and left Crissy alone when she was still a teenager, Crissy deserved a real home and someone to look after her for a change.

She did.

And Josie was happy for her.

She *was*.

But…

She couldn't stop the fear that it wouldn't be long before Crissy realized she didn't need Josie or the other Angels anymore. She had everything to make her happy right here in her little corner of Texas. And then where would Josie be?

Crissy had always been the driving force behind the Angels. Even before they'd started the fund-raisers, Crissy had been the one who organized their get-togethers. If she was suddenly too busy to bother, Josie could easily see herself and the other girls drifting apart.

A cold, empty feeling gathered inside her, settling like a cold fist in her stomach. She knew what would happen then. Since it was obvious she was never going to find Mr. Right, she'd be alone. Again. She closed her eyes, the icy fist squeezing harder.

She didn't want to go back to that lonely existence. She wrapped her hands around her mug, soaking up its warmth, doing her best to calm the gathering panic. She wasn't going to go back, dang it. She would work hard at the cowboy events, secure her position in the Angels. She'd be the best damned rodeo queen Texas had ever seen. She'd make herself indispensable. To the Alpine Angels *and* to Crissy.

The sound of the front door opening and closing

echoed through the house, followed by the thud of cowboy boots heading her way.

She jerked herself out of her reverie and glanced at her watch. Six-fifty. Braxton must be an early riser. And mucho dedicated to be here so early.

But it wasn't Braxton who darkened the kitchen door. It was Tommy Ray Bartel, looking tall and handsome—and a little bit irritated. He stopped just inside the kitchen, raked his gaze over her, shifted it to the paper on the table and lifted it back to her. "What in that newspaper is so damned important you're wasting half the day reading it?"

My, my, my, wasn't he on his high horse? She raised a brow. "Half the day? It's not even seven o'clock yet."

"The coolest part of the day is between sunrise and eight o'clock. And you're wasting it sitting here sipping coffee."

The coolest part of the day? She hadn't considered that. But still, she wasn't about to jump just to make him happy. He was still in the doghouse. She took a leisurely sip of coffee. "Unless I'm working, I try not to think of anything before noon as even being part of the day."

"*Noon.* It's hotter than hell's half acre by noon. Not to mention three-quarters of the day's gone by then."

She took another sip. "Not if you're up until after midnight it's not." And she quite often was. "And can the attitude, cowboy. If anyone's got the right to be snippy here, it's me."

His eyes narrowed on her. "Is that why you left me

standing in the corral twiddling my thumbs for the last two hours? Because you're still mad about the other night?"

"I left you standing there because it never occurred to me that anyone stood *anywhere* at five o'clock in the morning. Twiddling their thumbs or otherwise. But now that you've pointed out what an effective form of revenge it is, watch out for tomorrow morning."

Anger sparked in those blue, blue eyes, but he didn't snap back at her. He looked away, taking a deep breath, making an obvious effort to rein in his temper. Finally he met her gaze squarely. "All right, I misread the situation. It's just that you were pretty mad when we went our separate ways yesterday, and I have a sister who's into petty revenge. Making someone wait while she reads a book or does her nails is one of her favorites. I just assumed—"

"I'm not your sister," she snapped. And after the night they'd spent together, it rankled that he would put her anywhere near that category.

A ghost of a smile tugged at his lips. "No, you're not. I should have given you the benefit of the doubt."

"Yes, you should have."

Regret pulled at the corners or his mouth. "I meant it, you know, when I said I was sorry for the other night. I wasn't just blowing smoke to calm you down. I knew you were different than the women I usually drag off to hotel rooms the moment I met you. And knowing that, I should have walked away."

Different. She'd been different? Different in a good way? A ridiculous spark of hope flickered inside her. "How was I different?" She wanted to cut her tongue out the second the words were out of her mouth. But damn her ever-hopeful heart, she wanted to know if he'd felt something for her, something more than casual lust.

He ran a hand down his face, obviously unhappy with the direction the conversation was taking. "Look, the women I pick up are looking for the same thing I am, one night of sex. Pure and simple. You didn't seem the type. You were too…sweet. I should have just walked away."

"Why didn't you?"

He shook his head, guilt flashing across his face. "I don't know. I was drinking, feeling sorry for myself and—"

"So I was just a drunken mistake?" She couldn't keep the pain from her voice.

"No, it wasn't like that."

"It felt like that."

He closed his eyes, regret filling his expression. When he opened his eyes, the shadows she'd noticed that first night were back in force. "I'm sorry."

"So am I." But she'd learned early on feeling sorry for herself didn't get her anywhere. And there was a lot more at stake here than her bruised heart. This was the man who would teach her what she needed to know to secure her future with the Angels—and help Josie earn enough money for a little girl who needed a kidney transplant. They needed to get along. So she forced the pain away and made herself concentrate on the here and now. "Okay, cowboy, leave it in the past. What are you going to teach me today?"

He gave his head a single nod, accepting the offer of truce. "We're going to start with roping. And it's best we get a move on. The day's only going to get hotter."

"Good enough." She pushed up from the table and followed him out. The heat hit her the second she stepped onto the porch. Good Lord, it *was* already hotter than Lucifer's den. How did Texans stand it?

She followed Tommy Ray, doing her best not to notice his broad shoulders. Or his cute butt. Or the inexplicably sexy stride cowboy boots created. She dragged her gaze from him and sighed. Why were the off-limits ones always the cutest? And a man who wanted nothing more than a single night of sex was definitely off-limits.

The stiff new leather of her own cowboy boots rubbing against her heels, she trailed the man out to the pen he'd pointed out last night.

He strode through the open gate and stopped just inside. "Since calf-roping is the event that requires the largest number of skills—riding, roping, throwing the calf and tying him up—we're going to start there."

She took a quick glance around. A stack of six round, bright blue plastic canisters, about two feet wide and eight inches deep were set neatly beside the gate. A bale of hay with a black plastic calf's head stuck in one end sat in the middle of the corral. She stared at it. "That's what I'm supposed to rope?"

"For now."

"Doesn't look that hard."

"For someone as athletic as you, I'm sure it won't be." He stepped up to the blue canisters and tapped the top one. "These are the ropes. Eventually you'll pick one that suits you best. But today I thought we'd start with the top one. It's the smallest diameter, which I'm guessing will fit your hand the best. If it doesn't, we'll move on to something a little bit bigger." He opened the top container and removed a perfectly coiled rope.

"Wow, a rope in a hat box. Is that how you keep them from ending up in a heap of knots?"

He smiled. "Nope. That's your job. The rope can just keeps the rope in perfect throwing shape."

She raised a brow in question.

"A good cowboy—or cowgirl—can lasso a calf with just about any rope. But they're going to be faster and more accurate with a rope that has the perfect stiffness for them. The problem is, heat and humidity affect how stiff or soft a rope is. The heat makes a grass rope softer, the humidity stiffer. So once you find a rope that's got the best feel for you, you're going to want to keep it just that way. The rope cans do that for you."

Who'da thought? She tipped a shoulder. "All righty then, rope cans are my friends. Now what?"

He looked at her hands. "You didn't happen to bring any gloves with you, did you?"

She shot him a sideways glance. "You waited until we got out to the corral to ask that?"

He sent her a look of his own. "Does that mean you have them or you don't?"

"I don't."

"Okay, we'll make do today, but tonight you should get Crissy to take you to town and get you outfitted. Gloves," he glanced at her feet, "I see you've got the boots. How about a hat?"

She shook her head.

"You're going to need one of those, too. Especially if you're not going to practice before the sun's so high."

She grimaced. "Don't worry. You're right about the heat. It's pretty miserable already. I'll be out earlier tomorrow."

"Good. Let's get going."

He got points for not gloating about the heat thing. And for apologizing again for the other night. She suspected, if one dug deep enough, he was a decent guy. A decent guy who liked old cars—and understood about loneliness. She sighed. Too bad he had the sexual morals of an alley cat.

He moved off a few feet and faced her, the rope, arranged in neat coils, held in front of him. "There are only four things on a rope you need to remember. The eye." He pointed to a small noose at one end of the rope. "The horn knot, which is at the tail of the rope." He pointed to a small round opening obviously meant to fit over the horn of the saddle.

She listened as he finished his dissertation on the rope then showed her how to hold it, how to swing it, how to aim it and finally how to throw it over her target. But while she did her best to pay attention to the lesson, her gaze kept wandering to more interesting ground. Like the way his nimble fingers caressed the coils of twisted fibers. Or the graceful way his body moved as he swung the rope and tossed it toward the target. Or the downright sexy way he flicked the rope from the stationary calf's head and gathered it back up, like a man reeling in his lover.

He was pulling the rope in now. His hands worked quickly and efficiently, reminding her just how proficient they'd been stripping off her panties and placing her just where he wanted her on the bed.

He gathered the last stray coil. "Got it?"

She snapped her attention to his face, trying to ignore the heat washing over her. Heat that had nothing to do with the sun. "I think so." Great. Her voice was as rough as the gravel roads leading to this place.

Luckily, he didn't seem to notice. He held the rope out to her. "Give it a try."

She took the rope, making sure their fingers didn't connect. But the warmth from his hands still infused the rough fibers, reminding her how warm his touch had been. She ruthlessly pushed the thought away. She needed to concentrate. This was important. She tested the feel of the rope, swinging it gently back and forth. "It's a lot stiffer than I would have thought."

"That's because the few ropes you've handled have probably been for securing things, not roping things. The stiffness is what maintains the loop as it sails through the air. Without it, you'd be hard-pressed to lasso anything. Give yourself a minute or two, you'll adjust to the feel."

Nodding, she stepped far enough away that she wouldn't have to worry about hitting him when she started swinging.

"Get the size loop you want first."

Copying the actions he'd shown her, she held her hand straight out to her side and lengthened the loop until the end of it hit her leg midcalf.

"Good enough. Now give it a swing."

She stepped even farther away. The loop looked a lot bigger than she'd imagined. Confident she wouldn't hit anything, she started swinging.

Tommy Ray watched, his blue-eyed gaze sharp. "Not so wild with your arm, just twist your wrist, remember? And keep the hand you're swinging with close to your head."

Oh, yeah. She'd been so busy watching him, she'd only half heard his instructions. Bad. She had to get this right. Focusing on the task at hand, she quit rotating her arm and concentrated on circling her wrist to keep the rope moving.

"That's better. Now let's see you throw. Line up behind your target, aim at his head and release the rope as you send your hand toward the target."

She strode toward the hay bale and plastic head, keeping the rope turning. Tension tightened her grip. Silly. How hard could roping a stationary target be? Clearing her mind, she consciously relaxed her grip, locked her gaze on the calf's head, took two more swings, making sure she was properly lined up and let the rope fly.

It sailed through the air—and landed four feet to the right of the target.

"Oh, man. That wasn't even close." She obviously hadn't relaxed as much as she thought.

Tommy Ray chuckled. "No, it wasn't. But it wasn't bad for a first try. Just gather up your rope and try again."

"Not bad for a first try?" She looked at him as though he'd lost his mind. If she didn't do better than this, she was in big trouble.

He just tipped his head toward the roping dummy. "Try again."

She pulled the rope back, coiling it in her hand, her tension ratcheting up a notch. Once she had the loop swinging again, she stepped closer to the target, locked her gaze on the calf's head and sent her hand angling toward it once more.

The rope bounced off the calf's head and landed in a heap in front of the hay bale.

"Better. Again."

Maybe better, but it wasn't good. She gathered the rope and tried again. And again. And again. Each time the rope bounced off the dummy or missed him completely. She turned to Tommy Ray, frustration tightening every muscle in her body. "What am I doing wrong?"

He smiled, shaking his head. "What? Did you think you were going to pick up a rope and turn into Will Rogers?"

She scowled at him. "I thought I'd at least be able to drop the loop over his head."

"And with practice, you will. Try again."

But half an hour later she wasn't getting any better. In fact, she seemed to be getting worse. She was now missing the hay bale and the taunting black head more than she was hitting it. She turned to Tommy Ray with an accusing glare.

He had the audacity to chuckle. "Just take a breath. You're too tense."

Of course she was tense. Her future with the Angels depended on her ability to master these skills. And if this morning was any indication, she was going to suck at it.

"Relax," he coached. "Roll your shoulders, take a deep breath and try again. Try not putting so much power behind your swing. You can add the power once you have the motion down."

She turned back to the dummy. It wasn't just a bale of hay with a plastic head stuck in it. It was the spawn of Satan, sent here to bedevil her.

Well, she wasn't going to let it. She could do this. She *could*. She leveled her gaze on the black head. Rolled her shoulders. Took a deep breath. Swung the rope and threw.

It bounced off the big black ears sticking out to either side of the head. She looked back over her shoulder.

Tommy Ray was watching her, smiling.

That gut-wrenchingly sexy smile that made her stomach flutter and her palms sweat. "Quit smiling. It's annoying—and damned distracting."

He cocked a brow, his lips twitching, male pride flashing in his eyes. "Distracting, huh?"

He was obviously thrilled to death he could make her pulse pound with nothing more than a smile. She narrowed her eyes on him. "Don't look so smug. I could undo a button and have your pulse galloping, too. Then we could both be miserable, because there's no way I'm going to repeat what happened the other night."

His smile faded. "No. Let's concentrate on the roping. You released the rope a fraction of a second too late that time, so the loop closed down. Let go earlier. And—"

"*Don't* tell me to relax again. I am relaxed." At least as relaxed as she was going to get with so much at stake and Tommy Ray looking on. She plowed a hand through her hair. "Look, you've shown me how to do what I need to, now I just have to practice. It might be best if you go away while I do."

He hesitated, but only for a second. "Okay, I'll go.

God knows there's plenty of work on the range for me. But if you decide you need me later, just tell any one of the ranch hands. They'll send someone out to get me."

"I won't need you. I'm fine."

He grimaced, but gave his head a nod. "Okay." He strode toward the gate, but stopped halfway there. Striding back to her, he took his hat from his head— and dropped it on hers. "Keep that until you get one of your own."

The hat dropped down almost to her eyes as a faint wave of his spicy aftershave wafted down, reminding her just how good he'd smelled. And his heat, already saturating the hat's band, soaked into her head, reminding her just how warm he'd been as he'd lain over her, pushed into her. Reminders she did not need. She pulled it off and held it out to him. "I'm fine. And you need it as much as I do."

He shook his head, taking a step back. "I'm a lot more used to the sun and heat than you are. If you get heat stroke, Crissy'll have my head." He headed back to the gate. "I'll check on you later. See how you're doing."

She stared at the battered tan hat, debating whether or not to put it on. Wondering if Tommy Ray's heat would be more of a distraction than a protection. She looked up at the hot, burning Texas sun. Definitely the more imminent threat. She couldn't afford heat stroke. The rope was giving her all the problems she could handle.

She dropped the hat onto her head, ignoring the fact is was a size too big, ignoring the cowboy's heat soaking into her scalp and turned back to the dummy, gripping the rope's rough coils with dogged determination. If it took her all day and half the night, she was going to get this.

She had to get this. The only family she'd ever had was at stake.

Chapter Four

Tommy Ray stared into the night-darkened corral, watching the lone figure working in the circle of light created by one of the tall yard lights. He'd just gotten in from the range. It was late. As often happened when the moon was full, time had slipped away. He'd thought Josie would have headed in by now. But she hadn't. She was still trying to rope the ever-steady hay-bale calf.

Her shirt pulled tight over those luscious breasts as she swung the rope. Her jeans cupped her curvy little backside. Her long blond hair flowed down her back, reminding him how it had felt brushing his chest. His blood heated, bringing him to full-blown arousal in a single heartbeat.

Not good. But hardly a surprise. They *had* practically burned the hotel down the other night. He'd never met a woman who was as downright fun in bed as Josie. But the heat pounding through him was damned inconvenient. And a little scary.

He'd made a point in the last four years to restrict his liaisons to one night of hedonistic bliss. If he happened to find a lady who was just passing through, so much the better. That was why he haunted the highway bar. Having the women disappear from his life the next day was the ideal scenario. Not only did he avoid uncomfortable goodbye scenes, but if the women left town he wouldn't be tempted to prolong the bliss—no matter how good the sex had been.

But Josie Quinn wasn't going anywhere.

She was staying right here in his own backyard. Images of that night pounded in his head. Images of her lying beneath him. Images of her staring up at him with nothing but warmth and sweet communion in her eyes.

He closed his eyes and willed the images away. He wasn't going down the relationship road again. Once had been enough to tear his life apart.

He had other priorities now. And he couldn't afford to be distracted. Which meant he had to keep his libido—and that empty ache that filled his chest more and more often of late—in check. His goals fresh in his mind, he opened his eyes and looked at his watch. It was even later than he'd thought. He glanced back at Josie.

Angling her hand toward the dummy, she threw, but

she released too late again and the narrow loop bounced off the calf's head.

She was way too tense. He needed to find a way to get her to relax. He strode into the pen. "Enough, Josie. It's almost midnight. You can work on it more tomorrow."

"I know what time it is." Her gaze never leaving the roping dummy, she swung the rope again and threw.

The loop went wide, sliding off the edge of the hay bale. "Stop already. Your arm is tired." He strode over to her and took the rope out of her hands.

"I don't want to stop. I'm getting it."

If the last two throws he'd watched meant anything, she wasn't getting anything. And he didn't think she was going to until she relaxed a little. But he wasn't going to point that out.

He glanced at the rope. Several dark brown splotches caught his attention. One of them wet and sticky. Was that what he thought it was? He held the rope up so the light hit it better. "Oh, for crying out loud. Let me see your hands."

She tucked her hands behind her back. "Don't worry about them, they're fine."

He took hold of a wrist and pulled a hand from behind her back, flipping it palm-side up. Her palm was a mass of blisters on top of blisters. But the blistered skin had long since been peeled from her fingers, leaving them raw and bleeding. He huffed in disgust. "Yeah, I can see that."

She jerked her hand out of his grasp and boldly held it out. "They're my hands. Give me the rope."

He snorted at the demand. "They might well be your hands, but I'm the one responsible for getting you ready for the rodeo. And you're not going to be ready if you've worn the skin away to the bone."

She wiggled her fingers, her lips pressed into an uncompromising line. "Give it."

"No. And you can forget about practicing tomorrow or the next day, either. You get some bandages on those hands, let them do some healing and we'll talk about starting again the third day."

"I can't take three days off."

"I'm not giving you a choice. And just what in the heck, may I ask, possessed you to keep throwing until your hands were raw and bleeding?" He shook his head. Those poor delicate hands had to hurt like hell.

"They'll heal. But I *have* to get these skills down."

"And you will. But not in a single day."

She paced away, her brows pulled together in frustration and worry. "What if you're wrong? What if I can't get them? Not in a day or a week or a bloody year?"

She was wound tighter than the fibers in a rope. "Come on, give yourself a break. This is the first day you've ever held a rope. It'll come."

"What if it *doesn't?*"

"If it doesn't come, then it doesn't come. Calf roping is just one of the events at the rodeo. You're competing in four other events. If you don't get the roping down you'll make money in one of the others."

"Who says? What if I'm not any better at riding broncs or running barrels or—"

"Hey, take a breath. You're going to be fine. And getting every event perfect isn't crucial. There're going to be plenty of cowboys competing to help the Angels pull in the dough. Lily's going to be covered for her kidney transplant, no problem."

Her expression didn't lighten. "Yeah, I know she will. And I can't say how thankful I am for that. But unfortunately, Lily's not the only one with something on the line here."

He rocked back, studying her. "What's on the line for you? Your reputation as an athlete? Anyone who's seen you on a snowboard knows you have talent."

She waved away his comment. "I'm not worried about my athletic reputation. I'm worried about letting Crissy down."

"As long as you're trying your best you're not going to let Crissy down."

"Oh, please. You've known Crissy long enough to see how important the Angel charity is to her. If I don't make money, I'll let her down. And I'll lose her as a friend."

"Why on earth would you lose her as a friend?"

"Because five minutes with Crissy makes it pretty obvious she's planning to switch the alpine events to cowboy events. Events that can be hosted by the Big T.

Where, like you said, there are plenty of cowboys to make up for any inadequacies I or the other Angels might have. If we don't fit in, the last thing she's going to need is a ragtag bunch of women hanging on her coattails."

"Ragtag women? Is that what you're worried about? The financial disparities between Crissy and you guys now that Crissy has inherited the Big T?" He shook his head. "You're worrying about nothing. Crissy isn't the type who turns her back on her friends because her fortunes have changed. Or because they can't rope a calf."

"Maybe she would understand if I can't learn to rope a calf. But that doesn't mean I'll still have a place in her life. People change. They move on."

He knew all about people moving on. How painful it could be. How, sometimes, you couldn't do a damned thing about it. And giving her a Pollyanna song and dance maybe wasn't all that fair. "You're right, sometimes people do change. When that happens you just have to…move along, too." No matter how hard it was.

She shook her head, panic and fear filling her expression. "You don't understand. The Angels aren't just a bunch of girls I get together with now and then for a bit of fun. They're my family."

"Your family?

"Yes," she snapped.

He knew women's friendships were important to them, but… "What about your real family? Your mom, dad, brothers, sisters? What about them?"

She looked away, her lips pressed into a thin unhappy line, tension radiating from her like heat from a campfire.

Okay, so her family wasn't the subject to address if he wanted her to relax. Back to the original subject. "If the Angels have been the center of your life, maybe it's time to shift that focus. Create something that's just yours."

She shook her head. "It's not that easy."

No, it wasn't easy. He knew. And he wasn't at all sure she needed to do anything so drastic. "Look, if you're so worried about Crissy deciding she doesn't need her friends anymore, why don't you talk to her? Let her know what you're thinking, what you're worried about. See what she has to say."

She huffed in exasperation. "That's ridiculous. What do you think she's going to say? Yeah, you're right, I don't need you guys anymore. Crissy would never say that. She'd never think it. But that doesn't mean it wouldn't happen. Life has a way of pushing you in its own direction. And from my experience that direction is never good." Without another word she turned on her heel and strode away, her stride stiff and agitated.

He stared at her retreating back. Yeah, that had gone well. He'd relaxed her right up.

Chapter Five

The next night Tommy Ray led his horse into the barn. The sun had gone down about an hour ago. Most of the cowboys had headed home or to the bunkhouse a good hour before that. "Come on, son." He stopped Connor in front of the tack stall, dropped a rein to ground-tie him and pulled the saddle from his back. After depositing it on its rack, he grabbed a brush, collected Connor and led him into his stall.

As he started to brush, a faint voice drifted in from outside. He glanced toward the big open door at the end of the barn. He hadn't seen anyone wandering about when he'd come in, but someone was out there now.

Josie strolled in, the black, star-studded sky behind

her, her blond hair swinging gently on her shoulders, her breasts bouncing softly with her slow, easy gait.

His body shifted into overdrive. Pitiful. But apparently the way of things whenever the woman was within shouting distance. He forced his thoughts from the erotic images flashing in his head and lowered his gaze to her tummy.

She was holding the bottom of her shirt out from her, like a woman did with an apron when she was holding something in it. He was glad to see Josie was taking care of her hands. Soft gauze was wrapped around both palms and small flesh colored bandages circled most of her fingertips.

The bulge in her shirt said whatever she was carrying wasn't very big. But she was intent on it. "Hold on guys, we'll be with mommy in just a minute."

Be with mommy? "What have you got there?" he asked.

Josie startled, her gaze flying around the barn until she spotted him in the stall with Connor. Her shoulders slumped with relief. "You scared me. I thought the barn was empty."

"It was, a minute ago. I just got in from the range. So what do you have in your shirt?"

She walked over and tipped the edge so he could see.

"Ah, little kitties. Why aren't they with their mom?"

She tipped her head toward the hayloft that ran over the stalls on the other side of the aisle. "She's moving them. And with half the litter gone, it was dark and lonely in the old nest. They were mewing pitifully. So I thought I'd hurry things along. Plus, how pleasant can it be being dragged by the scruff of your neck halfway across Texas?" She held the shirt hem in one hand and stroked one of the tiny, furry plibs.

He smiled. "I think they're pretty used to being carried that way."

"Which doesn't mean it's any fun. And why make them go through it when I can carry them in luxury?"

It was the angel in her coming out. The sweet wholesomeness that had pulled at him at the honky-tonk. Hell, that still pulled at him. "Why indeed?"

At the end of the barn a gray tabby jumped down from the hayloft and started down the cement aisle. Her sagging teats gave her away as the kittens' mom.

He nodded toward her. "You better grab her before she goes out and finds an empty nest."

"You're right." Josie knelt down in the aisle. "Hey, mama kitty, I have your babies right here." She lifted one of the kittens.

The little mites couldn't be more than a week old. Their fur was thin, their faces were flat, their eyes were shut and their vocal cords were weak. But the tiny meow the kitten emitted was loud enough to catch the mom's attention as she trotted by. The tabby stopped in her tracks and snapped her head toward Josie.

Josie returned the kitten to her shirt. "See, I have them all." She tipped the edge of the shirt down so the cat could see. "Come on, we'll go put them away." She straightened and looked at him. "Well… Guess I'll see you tomorrow." She headed for the ladder at the end of the barn, mama cat hot on her heels.

He shouldn't follow her. Not with the way his body reacted any time she was near. It was tough enough being around her when he was teaching her. Putting himself in her company during social hours, during late-night social hours, was playing with fire. But…

She might need help getting those kittens up to the loft. He wouldn't want anyone to fall. He quickly left the stall, laid the brush aside and caught up with her. "I'll give you a hand with that."

At the bottom of the ladder, she glanced over her shoulder. "I can handle it." Keeping the kittens pressed safely to her belly with one hand, she steadied herself with the other and started up the ladder.

"I'll be right behind you…just in case you slip." The thought of having her in his arms once again sent another wave of desire through him.

But she made it to the hayloft without mishap.

He stood near the top of the ladder, watching her make her way toward the other end of the hayloft. He should go back to Connor's stall. But he didn't move.

He'd spent the day out on the range alone, and a little company to end his day would be nice. A warning voice in the back of his head told him to go to the bunkhouse if he wanted company. There would be plenty of men there who'd be up for a shot of something hard and some conversation. Maybe even a card game or two.

But who wanted to talk to a bunch of cowboys when a pretty lady was just a few steps away? He finished the climb to the hayloft and strode over to Josie, hay crunching beneath his boots.

She was hunkered down by a stack of hay bales, carefully placing kittens, one at a time, inside a small cavelike space between two bales. She put the last kitten inside the cozy space. "There you go, babies. All together again."

The kittens meowed and pushed toward each other, obviously distressed at their move and anxious to regain contact with one another. Their noisy efforts to regroup were haphazard and awkward, but it didn't take them long to form a writhing ball of fur. And once they were together, their anxious mews quieted.

Mama cat leaped onto the bale that sheltered her new hidey-hole, then jumped down with her babies. She nudged each kitten in turn, counting, he supposed, then settled down next to them offering nature's remedy for a baby's upset. Mother's milk. The fur ball moved en masse toward the goodies.

Josie chuckled, settling in the hay to watch the family reunion with satisfaction. She reached down and stroked the mama cat's head. "You're a good mom, aren't you, girl? You make sure everybody's safe, warm and well fed." There was a look in Josie's eyes, an appreciation for the mother's actions, that seemed to go clear down to her soul.

That look brought to mind the tension that had come

over her last night when he'd asked about her family, her tight-lipped refusal to even talk about them. "Why do I get the feeling that your mom wasn't such a good mother?"

She tensed, her hand momentarily stilling on the cat. But she quickly recovered, finishing the stroke on the mama cat's head and looking up at him, her expression smoothed into an emotionless mask. "I wouldn't actually know what kind of mother my mom was. She gave me up when I was three."

"Gave you up?" What the hell kind of mother gave up her child?

But Josie nodded. "Apparently it was too hard to juggle a kid, a job and her gambling habit. So she turned me over to the state. At least that's what the social workers told me when I got older and asked." She tried to sound casual, but there was nothing casual about the pain in her eyes.

Oh, man. "Where was your dad?" He sure as hell wouldn't have let any kid of his be turned over to the state.

She shrugged, another attempt at nonchalance. "I don't know anything about my dad. Who he was, what he did. My mother never put a name on my birth certificate. For all I know *she* didn't know who he was."

The picture was getting bleaker by the minute. No wonder she'd tensed up when he'd mentioned her family. "But you were adopted right?" Please let her have been adopted. By a loving, caring family.

She shook her head. "There aren't many couples who want older kids. And those who do usually don't want a child over two. I was three when my mom handed me over. And from what my social workers said, a handful."

His gut clenched. "So you were raised in a foster home?" He thought of the stories he'd heard on the news about foster homes. He hoped Josie's story had a happier ending than most of them did.

"A couple of dozen of them, actually."

"A couple of *dozen*?" That didn't sound good. Not good at all.

"In case you haven't heard, the foster-care system in this country is in crisis, has been for years. Too many displaced kids, not enough homes. Which means group homes are overcrowded or kids get put in homes that simply have an opening instead of in homes where they would fit in best. Which quite often makes a bad situation worse." A wry smile turned her lips. "And I was a problem child, remember?"

There had been no happy ending for sweet Josie Quinn. No wonder she didn't want the small kittens waiting in the dark alone while their mother moved them. She knew what it was like to be left alone, wondering where she was going to end up next. He wanted to pull her into his arms, chase the pain from her eyes, tell her she would never have to look for a home again.

That she'd never be alone again.

But he couldn't do that. He had things he had to do. Hearing about her childhood, however, made him understand better the exchange they'd had in the corral last night. "That's why the Angels are so important to you. Because they really are your family."

She glanced up at him. "That's what I told you last night."

"Yes. But I didn't get it then." He got it now. "You need to talk to Crissy, Josie. Let her know what you're feeling."

She looked away, pushing her fingers through her hair. "I'll think about it."

"I'd think pretty hard about it if I were you. Families are precious things. You wouldn't want to lose one over a misunderstanding that could be fixed with a simple talk."

Her lips pressed into a thin line. "No, I wouldn't."

"Then talk to her."

She blew out a long breath, obviously weighing the pros and cons. "Maybe I will."

"Good."

Her expression speculative, she turned her gaze on him. "And since you think talking is such a good thing, want to tell me why you think women are only good for one-night stands?"

He almost swallowed his tongue. "I beg your pardon?"

"You heard me."

"Yeah, I heard you. But that's not what I think."

"That's what you said the other day."

"I said, that's what *I* wanted out of a relationship, not that's all women were good for. I believe if such a thing ever crossed my mind, my mama would hand me my head on a platter, halved and broiled—extra crispy."

She smiled. "Yeah? I think I like your mama. Let me rephrase. Why is one night all you want from a woman?"

"What difference does it make?"

"It makes a difference because I think what happened in that room the other night was pretty extraordinary. Extraordinary enough that I'd like to know *why* you don't want anything more from a woman than one night of sex."

He took his hat off and scrubbed his fingers over his scalp. "Look, I don't have time for a real relationship right now. My one-night rule prevents anyone from thinking I'm making promises when I'm not."

"Oh, I see. It's not that you have anything against real relationships, it's just that you don't have time for one."

There was nothing accusatory in her tone. Nothing mean or snippy. She was just asking, sweetly, gently. So sweetly that if he refused to answer he'd look like a jerk. He gritted his teeth. "That's right."

"Hmm. Why don't you have time for one?"

No, nothing mean or snippy. Just sweet, dogged determination.

He needed to get the hell out of here. Before she had

him digging into all kinds of things he didn't want to dig into. "I just don't, all right? Why is really none of your business." He waved his hat toward the ladder. "I'd best be getting back to Connor. He'll be wondering where his late-night snack is." He turned on his heel and headed for the ladder. If he hurried he might still get away with his hide—and past—where they belonged.

"Does it occur to you," she called after him, her tone just as sweet, just as relentless, "that you made it my business when you followed me up to the hotel room, buried yourself deep, looked into my eyes and lied to me."

He stumbled to a halt.

He'd just had to follow her up here, hadn't he? She'd come by with the whole wholesome-goddess thing working and he'd followed her like a bull with a ring in his nose. And now she had him by another equally tender part of his anatomy.

Damn.

Josie watched him standing halfway between her and the ladder. She had him now.

He wasn't happy about it. A muscle in his jaw flexed rhythmically, tic, tic, tic, and every muscle in his body was tense. But he didn't move. Unfortunately, he didn't say anything, either.

So she pushed. "Why don't you have time for a relationship, Tommy Ray?" There was something between them. Something electric and promising and...

good. Something she was pretty danged sure he felt as strongly as she did. So why didn't he want to explore it?

He sighed, a short, frustrated sound. But finally he met her gaze head-on. "I don't have time for a relationship because I have a goal to meet. One that doesn't allow for any distractions."

"What kind of goal?"

He shot her a black scowl, trying to get her to back down.

But she just quietly waited.

He huffed again. "I have to make a million bucks, all right? That's my goal. To make a million dollars."

She rocked back on her hay bale. "You're kidding?"

He shook his head.

She stared at him, dumbfounded. "Well, you got me there. You didn't strike me as the kind of man who thought money was the most important thing in the world."

"The money's not for me."

"No? Who's it for?"

He looked away, that muscle along his jaw working again.

"Come on, Tommy Ray. If you make me drag every answer out of you, we'll be here 'til dawn."

He looked back to her, his expression unhappy but resigned. "It's for my boy."

"You have a son?"

He gave a single, short nod.

"Oh, my God." She snapped her gaze to his left hand, horrified at the thought she'd slept with a married man.

"Relax, there's no wife in the picture. Not anymore. Melissa left me four years ago."

Josie sighed in relief. Then realized how insensitive that must have sounded. "Sorry, I didn't mean to imply I was glad your marriage was over. Just that—"

"I know what you meant."

"Good." She shifted back to their previous conversation. "So, you have a boy?"

"Tommy Dean. He's six."

A sudden, unhappy thought hit her. "Is he sick? Is that why you need the money? Because if he is, the Angels—"

"He's not sick. He's a healthy little boy." Something dark and forlorn moved across his face. "As far as I know."

"As far as you... You don't know how he is?"

"I haven't seen him since he was two. When my ex and her new husband took him and moved to Spain."

"Spain? How the heck did that happen?"

"Easier than you think when new hubby is richer than Midas—and owns a villa outside Madrid."

A small light dawned. "Richer than Midas, huh? Is that why you want the million? Because Tommy Dean's stepfather has money?"

"Yes."

She could imagine how Melissa's husband's wealth

stung Tommy Ray's pride. But… "That's crazy, Tommy Ray. You don't need a fortune to visit your son."

"Yes, I do. Melissa's family has money coming out of its ears. And Melissa's new hubby is one of the richest men in Spain. I'd look like a damned fool showing up at the palatial estate my son's being raised on with nothing but a dirty pair of cowboy boots and a dusty hat."

"You are so wrong about that. Your son is not going to notice how dusty your boots are. He's—"

"Maybe not now. But as he gets older, he sure as hell will. And rodeo's a young man's sport. If I'm going to make that money, I have to do it now." His expression was hard, closed.

"You're not thinking straight, cowboy. If you develop a relationship with your son, he won't care how much money you have, now or ever. He'll know you love him. That's all that will matter."

Tommy Ray shook his head, desperation filling his expression. "That might be true of a kid raised in a normal household. But Tommy Dean isn't being raised in a normal household. He's being raised in the lap of luxury. Having an old man who barely has two nickels to rub together isn't going to do anything but shame him."

"*Shame* him? Whose words are those? Melissa's?" They had 'vindictive ex' written all over them.

"It doesn't matter whose words they are. They're true. I know. I saw the disdain on Melissa's parents' faces when they found out she was marrying a dirt-poor cowboy. I saw the disdain on her friends' faces when they came to visit us in the two-room house I could barely afford to *rent.* And I saw the look on Melissa's face when they left. It was shame. I won't do that to my boy."

She only had to look at the shame on Tommy Ray's face now to realize this picture was much more complicated than it appeared. She drew a deep breath and blew it out. "Your one-night rule isn't just about your son, is it? It's about Melissa, too. It hurt when you couldn't keep her in the style she was used to, didn't it?"

"Of course it hurt. What kind of man would I be if I didn't care if my wife was happy or not?"

"Not a very caring one, and I don't believe for a minute you were ever that. And now, because Melissa turned her back on you and took your son, you're gunshy when it comes to relationships. Understandable, but—"

"Oh, for— Is that what you think? That I don't want to get involved with another woman because I'm still hurting from Melissa?"

"It looks that way to me, yes."

"Well, it's not that way." His answer came hard and fast.

Too fast in her opinion. "Hmm."

"Look, I'm over her. Hell, I was over her long before she filed divorce papers."

She cocked her head, studying him, the tension in his lips, the deep unhappiness in his eyes. "You seem awfully angry to me, for a man who's over her."

He grimaced. "You're reading too much into this. Melissa was a rich socialite with some crazy romantic idea about cowboys and their lifestyle. That's what she saw in me, some fantasy. But it didn't take her long to realize that living on a cowboy's pay was anything but romantic. Our marriage was over before it even got started. And we both knew it."

"But you didn't get divorced right away. And Melissa was the one who asked for the divorce."

"Because Melissa got pregnant before we had the sense to break it off. And...I kept hoping things would work out." He shook his head. "Foolish. She came from wealth and luxury and I couldn't give her either."

For a man who was supposedly over his ex's betrayal, there was an awful lot of hurt and bitterness in those words. "You know, all women aren't as materialistic as Melissa. Nor are they looking for a man to provide for them. Most of us just want a man to share our lives with. Someone to celebrate the good things and help get through the bad things with. Someone to fix pancakes with in the morning and warm our beds on cold winter nights." She smiled. "And hot summer nights, too."

His nostrils flared at the sexual innuendo. But then he blinked and the only thing left was sadness. "And maybe one of these days I'll have the chance to find one of those women. Settle down. Have another child. But right now I have to concentrate on the son I have."

"I don't see how they're mutually exclusive. Why can't you chase after that ridiculous million and have a relationship, too?"

"Because I spend too many days of the year on the road to hold a relationship together, that's why. And because I need my brain in the game, not on some pretty filly. I can't be distracted. My son is too important." Blind determination shone in his eyes. "I want to be in his life. I'm going to make that money. And I'm going to make him proud. Now, if we're done with this little chat, I have a horse to feed." Without another word he strode toward the ladder, his steps long and powerful.

He was running hard now. She shook her head. She didn't doubt for a minute he believed he needed that million to see his son. He'd been deeply shamed by Melissa's parents' and friends' lowly opinion of his financial status.

But she also didn't doubt he was using that goal to hide behind. She wasn't sure he knew it. At least consciously. But it was clear as day to her. He wasn't over the pain Melissa had caused. He wasn't even close. And what better story to tell others—and himself—to protect his heart than that he couldn't get involved in any relationships because he was trying to get his boy back? Who could argue with that? It was the perfect excuse. One even he could believe.

She sighed, staring at the mama cat and her six babies. She wished she could make him see he was cheating his son. Wished she could make him see she wasn't anything like Melissa. But he was obviously not interested in seeing anything. He had his goal—and he was sticking to it.

Hearing his boots hit the cement floor below, she raised her voice so it would carry down to him. "You're making a mistake, Tommy Ray. A huge mistake. And everyone is going to pay. Me. You. And most of all, your son."

Chapter Six

Josie watched the brown Texas countryside fly by as she and Crissy sped down the highway in Crissy's big pickup. They were headed to Casey's Gulch for glove-and-hat shopping. But that was the last thing on Josie's mind.

She ran her hands over the brim of the hat in her lap, Tommy Ray's hat. She'd spent all night trying to get their conversation out of her head. But she couldn't. She glanced over at Crissy. "I was out at the barn last night, helping a mom move some kittens and…I ran into Tommy Ray."

Crissy looked over, her look dubious. "Yeah, what was he up to?"

"I think he was just quitting for the day, but…he told me about his son."

"Oh, yeah?"

Josie nodded.

"He tell you about his stupid million-dollar agenda?"

"Oh, yeah."

"That boy's got his head on so backwards it's amazing he can see where he's going."

Josie had to chuckled. "Yeah, I was thinking much the same thing." And it was too bad, because Tommy Ray Bartel might have had serious potential. Her fingers once again stroked the brim of his hat.

Crissy caught the movement. "Oh, God, that's Tommy Ray's, isn't it?"

Josie stilled, guilt heating her cheeks.

"Don't," Crissy warned. "Don't get attached to that thing or the man who owns it. He's dead set on his stupid agenda, and he isn't going to let anyone interfere with it. You let your emotions get tangled up with him, you're going to get hurt."

"He's hurting too, you know?"

"I do know. Or I can imagine, he's certainly never said he was hurting. But family's important to Tommy Ray. His mom and dad have nine kids. Five of them still at home. Tommy Ray rents a room above their garage just so he can help them out financially and be around to help with the younger kids. Losing his own wife and son had to hurt like hell. But he's chosen the wrong path to make his hurt go away, and he refuses to let anyone steer him to the right one. I'm not kidding, Josie. Don't get mixed up with him. He's a dead end."

Didn't she know it. "Don't worry. I don't have any misconceptions about Tommy Ray."

"Good. And please don't get that sad-puppy-dog look. There are a lot of other men in this world. Good, caring, *available* men."

"So I hear. Now if one of them would just fall into my path." She'd spent the first half of her life alone, she didn't want to spend the second half that way.

Crissy chuckled. "Don't worry, you're going to find, Mr. Right."

"I can only hope." She plowed her fingers through her hair and stared out at the empty Texas countryside.

Crissy glanced over at her. "You okay?"

"Yeah, I'm fine. I just…I don't know, sometimes I just think I need to get a life." And every time she reached for it, it seemed to slip through her fingers.

Crissy looked over at her, her brows crumpling together. "You have a life."

Josie grimaced. "Do I? It doesn't feel like I do."

"Well, you do. First off, twice a year you do the Angel events. That's having a life, Josie, and doing something important with it."

But she wasn't sure how much longer she'd be doing that. And then where would she be? "But that doesn't take much time. A couple of weeks out of the year. That leaves an awful lot of the year unaccounted for."

"This is about your job, isn't it? It's getting you down again."

She thought of the job she spent forty hours a week dragging her butt through. "It's part of it, yeah, but—"

"Look, I know being a legal secretary isn't your dream. But you do love the loft apartment it pays for. And that loft is the perfect place to chip away at your rocks, you've said so a thousand times. And stone sculpting *is* your dream. *And* you're getting closer to being able to support yourself with it. The last piece we auctioned off at our fund-raiser brought in big bucks. With pieces in three galleries, you'll be staying home and sculpting all day before you know it."

Being able to stay home and work on her sculpture had been her dream. But… "I'm not sure sculpting's what I want anymore."

Crissy's gaze snapped from the highway, locking onto Josie. "But you love sculpting."

"I do. I just don't know if I want to be home by myself all day doing it." Ever since Crissy had moved to Texas Josie's life had been a lot quieter. Too quiet. Working at home alone no longer held the appeal it once had.

Crissy fixed her gaze back on the road, one finger tapping impatiently on the wheel. "Okay, where is this coming from? What's going on?"

Last night Tommy Ray had pushed her to talk to Crissy. Pushed her to let her friend know how important their friendship was. She took a deep breath, blew it out and plunged ahead. "I miss having you in Colorado. I miss our evening phone calls when we'd catch up on each other's days. And I miss the weekends we used to spend together shopping, going to the movies and whatever else came to mind."

Guilt flashed across Crissy's face. "I haven't been calling enough, have I?"

"I'm not trying to make you feel guilty. I know you call as often as you can. I know the ranch is big and that you're learning everything from scratch and that you want to spend as much time with your new husband as you can. God knows, if I had a hunk like that in my life, phone calls are the last thing I'd have time for."

"It does get hectic sometimes, but I should have called more. Truth is, I miss those end-of-the-day calls, too. And our little get-togethers. Unfortunately, it was a lot easier for us to get together when I lived in Denver and you lived in the Springs than it is now with you in Colorado and me in Texas."

Things change in people's lives, and they move on.

Josie's chest tightened as she remembered the words she'd spoken just a couple of nights ago. "Yeah, it is."

The hum of tires sounded in the cab as the truck hurtled down the black asphalt.

"Well, ya know…" Crissy's expression turned thoughtful, her fingers once again tapping on the steering wheel. "You could move to Texas."

"What?"

A smile started to bloom on Crissy's face. "Move to

Texas. Why didn't I think of that earlier? It would be great. You could move here and work on the Big T. We could see each other even more than we did when we were both living in Colorado."

The idea zipped through Josie. But... "I don't know. I'm not going to be good at this cowgirl stuff and—"

"So don't be a cowgirl. We have lawyers in Texas, too. You could keep being a legal secretary until your sculptures are paying your way."

"Yeah, I could. But there's more to it than that. There's the Angel thing. I don't know if I can keep being an Angel if you change the venue to cowboy-type events. It's not looking real hopeful that I'm going to be good at this stuff." She took a deep breath and pushed the words she was most afraid to say out of her mouth. "And you may not want me around then."

"Oh, come on. You can't possibly know how good you're going to be at the rodeo events after one day— no matter how badly it went the other day. And what the heck do you mean, I won't want you around?"

Josie stared at the countryside sliding by, feeling awkward and self-conscious.

Crissy looked over. "You're not seriously afraid we won't be friends if you aren't part of the Angels, are you?"

All the fear of the past few months churned in her stomach. "Maybe."

Crissy shot her a hard look. "Well, that's the most ridiculous thing I've ever heard. We were friends before we were the Angels, and we'll be friends long after. Correction. We were *family* before the Angels, and we'll be family long after."

Josie stared at the dry, empty countryside. "Even families move apart."

Crissy took a deep breath. "Yeah, sometimes they do. But they don't have to. I think it depends on what the family wants. Personally, I don't want to lose any of you guys. And it doesn't sound to me like you want to lose me, either. So move to Texas. There's an old empty barn behind the new one. The ground floor would make the perfect sculpting studio, and you could do whatever you want with the top half to make it your home. Or you could pick a place on the ranch to build. In the meantime, you could stay in the big house."

She liked the idea. A lot. But… "I don't want to invade your life." God knew she'd been an unwelcome guest in almost every foster home she'd ever been in. She didn't want to spend her adult life in the same boat.

Crissy locked her gaze on Josie. "You could never invade my life. But if you moved here, you could enrich it."

One look at Crissy's expression convinced Josie her friend wasn't just saying the polite thing, Crissy wanted Josie on the ranch. Joy warmed her.

"Come on," Crissy prompted. "What do you have to lose?"

She wanted to jump on the invitation. But was it that easy? She ran her hands over the brim of the hat in her lap. Tommy Ray had said to speak to Crissy, but he'd also told her to create something that was just hers. And she thought that advice was as good as the other. The last thing she wanted was to move here and be a needy thing Crissy had to take care of. So...could she create something for herself here? "I like the idea of having a building as big as a barn for my studio," she thought aloud.

"It would give you a lot more room to work in than you have now," Crissy said, doing her best to sell the idea.

"It certainly would. I could have more than one project going at a time. And I'd have room to store extra pieces of stone. Which means I wouldn't have to let someone else snatch up the best hunks. I could buy them and keep them until I was ready to use them."

Crissy's eyes twinkled. "And think how nice it would be to have a living space that wasn't part of your studio."

"Yeah, no stone chips to cut my feet when I get up in the middle of the night. No gritty dust coating every surface of my apartment. I could live with that." Boy, could she live with that.

"And since you'll either be buying the place or renting it from me, we can make your payments flexible. Very flexible. That way you can use the nest egg you've been saving for the past few years for the renovations you need right away to make the place livable and to keep groceries on the table until money from the sculptures really kicks in."

Oh, no, she wasn't looking for a free ride. She paid her way in this world. She opened her mouth to protest.

Crissy cut her off. "Come on, Josie, it's not like I need the money. The Big T keeps me more than solvent, and you know it. And I'm not going to give you the place, I know you'd never accept it. We're just going to make your payment schedule flexible. Which means you wouldn't have to work on the ranch or go to work at another law firm unless you wanted to. You could work full time on your sculptures. And your worries about being home alone all day would be history. You get lonely, I'll be within a stone's throw. And so will a hundred-plus cowboys who would be more than happy to keep you company." Crissy waggled her brows.

Josie chuckled. "I hadn't thought of that."

"But you're thinking about it now, aren't you?" Crissy smiled wickedly.

"Maybe." It had a certain appeal. But cowboy's weren't the biggest draw. Keeping her family together was. And, who knew, maybe Mattie and Nell would find a move to Texas advantageous, too.

"So?" Crissy prompted.

"So…I like it. The more I think about it, the more I like it." Excitement sent the corners of her mouth soaring. "When can I look at the barn?"

Crissy's smile was just as big. "How fast can you pick out a pair of gloves and a hat?"

"How fast can you get us there?"

Crissy pressed the gas pedal closer to the floor.

Five minutes later they turned off the highway and headed down a smaller road that led to a small outcropping of houses and businesses.

Crissy slowed down at they approached the small town. "So, you interested in reeling in any of the other cowboys on the ranch?"

Josie shook her head, laughing. "What? I don't even get a week to get cute, classic-car-loving Tommy Ray out of my system?"

"Maybe another man, one with his head screwed on straight this time, is the best way to get him out of your system."

"Maybe, but who's to say the next one will be any better?"

Crissy chuckled wryly. "Now there's the rub. After six thousand years of civilization one would think we'd have come up with a better way than trial and error to separate the good from the bad."

They'd hit the one-block main street. Small businesses lined both sides of the street. One colorfully painted sign, sitting in front of a small, equally brightly painted building, caught her eye.

Find Your Perfect Mate!
The Best Dating Service In Town!

Josie smiled. Maybe there was a better way. And maybe Crissy was right. Maybe another man was the best way to get Tommy Ray out of her head.

Chapter Seven

Tommy Ray headed toward the big house. Today had been Josie's third day of healing, and he needed to see how her hands were doing. See if she could get back to cowgirling tomorrow.

He climbed onto the wide, wraparound porch, glancing at his watch. A little past seven. No doubt Josie would consider it past business hours, so he knocked instead of just walking in.

Mixed emotions swirled inside him. He'd studiously avoided her since the night in the hayloft. She'd cornered him, made him think about things he'd buried long ago. Made accusations that just weren't true.

You seem awfully angry to me, for a man who's over it.

Of course thinking about Melissa made him angry. She'd taken his dreams of a wife and family and crushed them beneath the stiletto heel of her Guccis. Guccis he hadn't been able to buy for her so she'd gone to her father for them. And then after she'd made sure he knew what a no-account bum he was, she'd taken his child and moved halfway around the damned world. What man wouldn't be angry?

But that didn't mean he wasn't over her. He was. As a matter of fact if he was any more over her, he wouldn't even remember her name. His million-dollar goal didn't have anything to do with Melissa, it was about his son. End of discussion.

But despite Josie bringing up uncomfortable memories and making ridiculous accusations, he couldn't get her out of his mind.

The door swung open.

And there she was. Sweet Josie Quinn, a thin silky dress covered in tiny flowers skimming over her lush curves, her usual straight curtain of hair groomed into a riot of cascading curls, her pretty bare feet slid into a pair of sexy, spiky-heeled sandals.

Desire pounded through him. She looked hot enough to send his blood pressure soaring. But… "What are you all dressed up for?"

"I'm going out."

He didn't like the sound of that. He strode into the foyer, his boots echoing on the shiny wood floor. "Going out where?" If she'd been wearing jeans and a cute little top, he'd figure she'd be out for a night with Crissy. But she wasn't going out with Crissy in that sexy little number.

The saucy hemline was barely long enough to be decent, the low neckline barely high enough, and the tiny spaghetti straps holding the thing up didn't even qualify as a momentary hindrance. No way was she dressed for a night out with the girls.

She hung a hand on her tiny waist—small bandages still covering the ends of her fingers—and cocked a curvy hip. "Out to a movie and a nice dinner with a very nice man from what I hear. Got a problem with that?"

Hell, yes, he had a problem with that. He knew what happened when she wandered into a place with nothing more on her mind than having a drink. The thought of what would happen on a *date* made him crazy. "Well, you don't let any grass grow under your feet, do you? And what do you mean, 'a very nice man from what you've heard'? You've never met the man you're going out with?"

"Nope. Not yet. I joined a dating service."

"A dating service? Oh, for… Patricia Lynn's Find Your Perfect Mate dating service?" Horror curled in his gut.

"That's the one. And—"

"For crying out loud, that woman's crazy. You let her find you a man, you'll be wandering off with some pervert."

She shot him a disparaging look. "I *like* Patricia

Lynn. She's smart and savvy and knows what she wants in a man. A trait I admire. And as luck would have it, she said she knew just the guy for me and was able to set this date up right away."

"If she's so good at picking out men, she'd have one hanging on her arm. And I've never seen one. So I'd think twice about any man she was able to lasso, if I were you."

"Maybe you haven't seen her with a man because she's not interested in just any man. She's looking for the *right* man to hang on her arm. A concept that is getting closer and closer to my heart."

"Her unattached status doesn't have anything to do with her selectiveness. It has to do with the fact she's a man-hunting piranha."

Josie lifted a single, imperious brow. "What is this, cowboy? You certainly can't be a jealous boyfriend. You made it pretty clear you weren't interested in that role, remember?"

He remembered. And he *wasn't* interested in being anyone's boyfriend. Not until he had that million, anyway.

An uneasy ache squeezed his chest. Even that might be a little early for jumping into a relationship. After all, once he had the money he should concentrate on building a relationship with his boy. *Then* he could start thinking about being somebody's boyfriend.

But while he had no desire to put himself in the boyfriend role at the moment, he didn't want anyone else in that role, either. Not with Josie. Ridiculous and unfair, but there it was. "Who did Patricia Lynn set you up with?"

"Ned Parsons. Who, she assures me, is a very nice man. And a hell of a catch, apparently," she added with a sugary-sweet smile.

Raw jealousy gnawed at his hide. He knew Ned. Hell, everybody knew Ned. He worked over on the Rocking M—and was the biggest ladies' man around.

"Am I interrupting anything?" The deep male voice came from the door Tommy Ray had left open when he'd stormed in.

Tommy Ray turned to see Ned Parsons standing in the portal.

Ned had on his going-out-to-dinner hat, his Saturday-night dancing shirt and his good boots.

And he was holding a small bouquet of flowers.

Oh, yeah, that boy had his moves down pat. Only a supreme act of will kept Tommy Ray from snarling at the man.

But before he had a chance to do anything, Josie walked around him, focusing her attention on her suitor. "Ned?"

Ned's eyes traveled from the top of her head to the tips of her toes, a slow smile of appreciation spreading across his face. "Yes, ma'am. You must be Josie. These are for you." He held out the handful of flowers.

Tommy Ray rolled his eyes.

But Josie's expression brightened as she looked at

the posies. "How lovely. Thank you." She took the flowers, held them to her nose and sniffed. "Beautiful. Come on in while I put them in some water. Then we can be off."

As Josie disappeared into the kitchen, Ned stepped into the foyer and tipped his head toward Tommy Ray. "Tommy Ray."

"Ned." Tommy Ray stared at the cowboy who was so obviously dressed to impress, his jealousy burning a hole the size of Texas in his gut.

The sound of cabinets being opened and closed followed by the sound of running water drifted from the kitchen.

Was he really going to just stand here and watch her walk out with Ned Parsons? The ugly truth was that it was the only choice he had. He didn't have any claim on the woman, couldn't have any claim on her, and she'd passed the age of consent.

But that didn't mean he couldn't do his level best to make sure nothing more interesting than a few dismal how-are-ya's happened on this little date. He leveled a stern look at Parsons. "She's got to be up bright and early tomorrow. Don't keep her out late."

Behind him, heels clicked against the wooden floor as Josie returned from the kitchen. Hearing his comment, she huffed in disgust, strode over to Ned, laced her arm through his and snuggled up close. "Don't let him bother you, Ned. Crissy put him in charge of teaching me how to rodeo and suddenly he thinks he's my keeper. But we're all grown up. We can decide how we handle the night." She smiled up at the local Romeo with a smile meant to melt men's hearts—and stoke their libidos.

Ned closed his hand over Josie's where it rested on his arm and smiled into her eyes. "Well, he needn't worry. I plan to take very good care of you."

Tommy Ray clenched his fists and gritted his teeth and willed himself not to pull Josie off Ned's arm and toss the overconfident cowboy out on his ass. He had no right interfering in Josie's love life. But the herd of angry bulls that had suddenly taken residence in his belly didn't like it. Not one damned bit. Still, he managed to keep his feet glued to the floor while Ned and Josie said goodnight and headed out.

Right up until the moment he heard Ned's truck growl to life and head down the road, the sound of crunching gravel marking its departure. Then he hurried out of the house and across the paddocks to his own pickup. Jerking the truck's door open, he jumped in. But he froze with his hand over the keys in the ignition. What the hell did he think he was going to do? Follow them to town? Shadow them on their date?

He'd look like a damned fool. And Josie'd probably have him arrested as a stalker. He ran a hand down his face, swearing viciously.

Women.

The first one he'd let himself care about had torn his heart from his chest and left with it still beating in her hand. And now this one, with her sweet, wholesome sexiness, made him want more than he could have. Made him remember that he'd once dreamed of a family of his own. Once dreamed of waking every morning with a warm, loving woman next to him. Once dreamed of children's voices echoing through the house.

But his ex had shattered that dream into a million tiny pieces. Now, his only hope was to recapture the one piece he couldn't live without. And he couldn't do that if he let Josie Quinn sidetrack him.

He should go home to the little room over his parents' garage, and forget about Josie. He'd promised his dad he'd work on the front porch. After thirty years of hard use, the wide wooden porch was on its last legs.

But he didn't move.

He wanted to know when Ned brought Josie home. Wanted to make sure any good-night kiss the boy had planned stayed respectable. Wanted to make sure the boy didn't follow her into the house, up to her room. *That* wouldn't be stalking. Just making sure good ol' Ned minded his p's and q's—and that Josie got plenty of sleep so she'd be bright-eyed and bushy-tailed tomorrow morning.

Yeah, he was just doing his job.

He tapped his fingers on the steering wheel. He had a new horse he could work. That would keep him from sitting here and gnashing his teeth for the next few hours. He climbed out of the truck and headed for the barn.

But five hours later he had to admit nothing was going to make him forget Josie was out with another man. He'd worked with the new horse, his old horse, two of the ranch stock and then he'd brushed every damned animal in the barn. But the picture of Ned with Josie hadn't left his head for a second.

The bulls that had moved into his gut were getting more restless by the minute. His stomach lining was wearing damned thin, as were his nerves. He strode to the end of the barn for the thousandth time in the last hour and looked to the dark outline that represented the hills surrounding the Big T. He willed Parsons' truck to drive through the small break in the pointy mounds.

But he saw nothing but darkness. And that darkness reminded him just what couples often did in the dark. He glanced at his watch. Almost midnight. The movie had gotten out two hours ago. Where the hell were they? And why the *hell* hadn't he followed?

Suddenly, a pair of headlights popped out from behind the hills. He squinted. Yep, Ned's pickup.

About damned time.

He doused the lights in the barn and made his way to the stand of cedars beside the big house's porch. He'd stashed his pickup behind the barn where it wouldn't be seen as long as Ned stayed on the main road winding through the corrals. He hunkered behind the pines where he wouldn't be spotted unless he needed to make his presence known.

He shook his head. She was turning him into a man who skulked in the shadows. Great. But he wasn't budging.

Parsons parked in front of the house and ran around the front of the pickup to open the door for Josie. He offered her a hand down and walked her to the door, his hand resting at the small of her back.

Tommy Ray gritted his teeth. The man didn't have to paw her, she was right there by his side, for crying out loud.

On the porch, they turned to face each other, Ned settling his hands on her shoulders and running a finger up and down her neck. A man positioning for a kiss.

The bulls in Tommy Ray's gut threatened to stampede. Only a supreme act of will kept them contained. A peck on the cheek he could live with. A quick peck on the lips, maybe. Anything more than that, he was shutting them down.

Lowered intimately, their voices floated over the night air. And then Ned dipped his head, his lips brushing over Josie's.

Tommy Ray clenched his fists, but he managed to stay put. Okay, buddy, you've kissed her. Now go home.

But the man didn't go home. In fact, he leaned down for another kiss. An openmouthed kiss.

That's it. Tommy Ray straightened from the shadows and strode toward the porch. "So, how was the movie?" He managed to keep his voice casual as he leaped onto the wooden porch.

Ned straightened, his gaze narrowing on Tommy Ray. Dropping his hand to Josie's waist, he shrugged. "With a pretty lady sitting next to you, who watches the movie?"

The herd in Tommy Ray's gut doubled. He straightened his shoulders and stepped forward, crowding Ned. "Well, the movie's over now so you can get along home. Like I said, Josie's got an early morning tomorrow."

"Oh, please," Josie muttered. "This is ridiculous."

Ned straightened to his full height and took a step closer to Tommy Ray. "I think the lady can decide when she needs to get to bed."

With a *tsk* of exasperation Josie stepped between them. "Okay, that's all the machismo I can stand." Pointedly turning her back on Tommy Ray, she looked at Ned and laid a hand on his chest. "I had a lovely evening tonight and I hope we'll do it again, but let's call it a night, shall we?"

Ned cast a concerned look over her head at Tommy Ray. "You sure you're going to be all right?"

"I'll be fine, really." She pushed up on her toes and gave his cheek a kiss. "Thanks again for the lovely evening."

He gave her a single nod. "My pleasure. You have a good night." He pinned a narrow-eyed look at Tommy Ray. "I'll be calling first thing tomorrow morning to see how she is. I wouldn't give her any grief if I were you." With a final glower, he strode toward his truck.

Josie watched him go then shifted her gaze to Tommy Ray. Crossing her arms over her chest, she glared at him expectantly.

Was she waiting for an apology?

Good luck. "Don't look at me like that. You do have to be up early tomorrow. Besides, is that the kind of man you're looking for? One who leaves at the first sign of trouble?"

She scowled at him. "You were not hiding behind those trees because you were concerned about me getting enough sleep. And he didn't leave at the first sign of trouble. He left because I asked him to."

He ignored the hiding bit. "I wouldn't have left you. Not with another man lurking around."

Her eyes popped wide. "You *did* leave me. Snuck away like a thief in the night, remember?"

"That…was different. I *had* to leave."

She looked heavenward and shook her head. "Okay, this is the stupidest conversation I've ever had. We're done here." She turned away, reaching for the door.

It *was* a stupid conversation. She had every right to do whatever she damn well wanted. He should let her go. But before she could open the door, the question that was tromping around in his gut burst out of his mouth. "Did he kiss you?"

She looked back to him, tossing a hand in exasperation. "You know he did. You were obviously watching."

He shook his head. "Not then. I made sure he didn't go too far that time. I meant earlier. While you were at the movies."

Indignation filled her expression. "*That* is none of your business."

"Did he?" he demanded.

Her eyes narrowed to little gray slits, and she tipped her chin up and looked down her nose again. "What if he did?"

The horny bastard *had.* Kissed her and God knows what else in the cloaking darkness of the theater.

The bulls broke lose.

He closed the distance between them. And then his lips were on hers, hard and demanding. He was going to wipe every thought of Ned Parsons from her head.

She startled and even, for a second, tried to push him away. But then her hands fisted in his shirt and she was kissing him back.

The same heat and need that had exploded between them the night they met flared again. Hotter. Wilder. He pulled her closer, drinking in her softness, reveling in the sharp urgency of her response.

She rose up on her toes, opening to him, trying to get more of him.

Yes. By the time he was done she wouldn't even remember what's-his-name.

But suddenly she was pulling her lips from his and pushing him away. "Stop it. You can't do this." She stumbled away, her breathing hard and fast. "You can't have it both ways, Tommy Ray. Either you want me or you don't. But you can't say you're not interested and then pull this crap."

He drew in deep breaths of air, trying to cool the frustration pounding through him. She was right. This was crazy. As he'd pointed out to himself earlier, he wasn't playing fair. But he couldn't stand by and watch her go out with other men, either.

He *couldn't*. And…

Maybe he didn't have to. Maybe he was making this way more complicated than it had to be. "If you're so set on dating someone while you're here, date me."

Her brows winged toward her hairline. "What happened to your one-night rule?"

What indeed? It seemed to be blowing away like a feather in a storm. Not good. But stopping it was beyond his ability. "It doesn't apply here. That rule prevents anyone from thinking promises are being made when they're not. But you know my agenda. You know I'm not promising forever after. And realistically, why would you want that from someone here in Texas, anyway? When the rodeo is over, you'll be heading home. Getting back to your job and life in Colorado. So there's no reason we can't enjoy this…this thing that's between us. And when you head back to Colorado, it's over."

She smiled, a rather sad smile. "But I'm not heading back to Colorado. I'm staying here."

Surprise flashed through him. "You're staying?"

She nodded. "I'm buying the old barn from Crissy. I'm going to turn the top floor into an apartment and the bottom floor into a sculpting studio."

Surprise washed over him. "You sculpt?"

Another smile, this one with a wry twist. "We don't

know a lot about each other, do we? For a couple who's been to bed together."

No, they didn't. But he wanted to know more about her. A lot more about her. A reality that should have sent him running for his truck. The last time he'd wanted to get to know a lady more, she'd torn his world apart.

When he didn't say anything, she went on. "Yeah, I sculpt. Stone. I started when I was pretty young, really. Fifteen. One of the foster dads I lived with for a while was a stone sculptor. He got me started and I fell in love with it. The process of carving life out of an emotionless block. An end product with the ability to last through the aeons. I've always hoped someday to be able to make a living at it. Now, with a little creative financing, Crissy's giving me that chance."

"So you're moving along. And managing to keep your family, too. Good for you." He was happy for her. Thrilled for her. But her decision to stay complicated the hell out of his brilliant idea.

He paced away, trying to wrap his brain around her news. Part of him told him to walk away while things were relatively simple and uncomplicated. But another part of him, the part that had been in upheaval since she'd wandered into his life, wouldn't budge. "Okay, that complicates things. But it doesn't have to put an end to them. We're both adults. As long as we both know going in that nothing serious is going to come of this, I don't know why we couldn't pick up where we left off at the honky-tonk."

She shook her head. "No one's ever made my blood sing as sweetly as you, Tommy Ray. But I'm not interested in a fling. I want what I never had growing up—a real home, a real family. I deserve that. And this time, I'm not settling for less."

She deserved to have it all. But where did that leave him?

In the same cold, lonely place he'd been for the past four years.

Chapter Eight

"He did what?" Crissy dropped into her father's leather chair on the business side of the desk.

Josie dropped into one of the chairs on the opposite side. "You heard me." It was pushing nine o'clock, later than she'd vowed to start practicing in this Texas heat, but she hadn't been up to the day at dawn. Not after spending half the night staring at the ceiling thinking about last night—and Tommy Ray's kiss. So she'd sent a message out to the barn that she'd be out later and tried, futilely, to catch a few more z's.

"He chased Ned away? And kissed you?"

Josie nodded, remembering the electric kiss Tommy

Ray had delivered last night, fresh heat washing through her.

"Okay, that's it. I'm going to kick that boy's butt. What was he thinking?"

"I think we both know what he was thinking. He wanted me to compare whatever happened between Ned and me to what happened between me and him—and he intends for Ned to come up short."

Crissy made a face. "And it worked, didn't it? He wiped thoughts of Ned right out of your head."

Josie looked away sheepishly. "I have to say with their kisses coming one on top of each other that way…"

Crissy huffed in exasperation. "Don't let him do this, Josie. Ned Parsons is a good man. A very good man. He's solvent. He's dependable. He's kind. He's handsome. *And he doesn't have some screwy agenda he's chasing.*"

"Tommy Ray's not chasing his screwy agenda, he's hiding behind it."

"I'm aware of that. But I don't think he is. And he's not going to give it up, Josie."

No, she didn't think he was. But she wished he would. She wished there was a way to make him see he should.

Crissy jabbed a finger at her. "*Don't* get that look."

Josie did her best to look innocent. "What look?"

"*That* look. That even-though-it's-obvious-as-hell-to-me-and-everyone-I-know-that-he's-the-worst-man-

I-should-be-getting-mixed-up-with-I-want-to-give-him-a-chance-anyway look."

Josie had to smile. "I can't help it. He's—"

"A train wreck waiting to happen. *Forget* him, Josie. He's not going to make you anything but crazy. And sad. Think about Ned. He's a bit of a player right now, but I know he's looking to settle down. And you couldn't find a nicer guy."

Josie sighed. "You're right. Ned *is* a nice guy. But he's not the one." Tommy Ray's kiss had made that more than clear.

Crissy growled. "I am going to strangle Tommy Ray the next time I see him. In the meantime, maybe you ought to forget about the entire male population for a while. Concentrate on your new home."

Warm fuzzies filled her. The barn was going to make a great home. Not just a great place to stay, but a great *home.* A place with family close at hand.

Maybe putting men on the back burner for a while wasn't such a bad idea. There was certainly plenty else going on in her life right now. She didn't need to borrow trouble. And men were always trouble.

She looked to her friend. "I want to thank you again for thinking of the barn. For inviting me here. I can't tell you what this means. A house of my own…" Words failed her.

Crissy smiled gently. "Hey. I know what it means. I didn't have a home before I came here, either, remember?"

Tears stung her eyes. Good tears. But still, she swiped at them before she made a spectacle of herself. "So, know any good contractors? I can't afford to do a lot right away, just the necessities. A bathroom, kitchen. But I'd like to get those in as soon as possible."

"I don't personally know any. But I'm sure Tate knows a few. I'll ask him and let you know."

The sonorous chimes of the doorbell reverberated through the office door.

Muffled cowboy boots on the wooden floor told Josie that Braxton was getting it. Then, more than one set of footsteps headed for the office. She and Crissy looked to the office door just as someone knocked on the oak panel.

"Come on in," Crissy called.

The door swung open and Braxton walked in trailed by a woman and a small girl.

The woman wore an austere gray business suit and looked to be in her forties. Despite her dour dress, she had an open, friendly smile and a twinkle in her eyes.

The small girl bringing up the rear wasn't tricked out quite so neatly. Her well-worn blue jeans were a good size too big for her tiny body. The cartoon character on her T-shirt was so faded one could barely make it out. Even the big paper bag she was clutching so tightly had seen better days. And she didn't look nearly so sparkly. She looked small and vulnerable and...frightened.

Braxton waved a hand toward the older woman. "Crissy, this is Marilyn Turner from the Department of

Child Services. And I believe you've already met this young lady." He waved toward the small girl, giving her a big smile.

A smile broke out on Crissy's face, as well. "Hey, Lily, what a nice surprise. What are you doing here?"

Lily?

The girl they were raising funds for?

Although Crissy had met the child, Josie and the other Angels hadn't. All Josie knew about her was what Crissy had told her. She was six years old, had kidney failure from meningococcal septicaemia—and she was in the foster-care system. Had been since her mother had abandoned her when she was four.

Josie studied the small child. She'd certainly been named appropriately. She looked like a tiny, delicate lily with her pale skin and the freckles sprinkled across her nose. Her heart aching for the waif, Josie dropped her gaze to the paper bag in the tiny, clenched fist. Crissy might not know what the girl was doing here, but Josie did.

How many times had she been shuttled from one foster home to the next, what few possessions she had shoved into a paper bag? And she'd been a healthy child—granted a difficult one sometimes—but still…. This child with her serious health problems had probably been shuttled to twice the number of homes Josie had.

"Well," Ms. Turner began. "We're here because we ran into a little glitch this week with Lily."

Concern knitted Crissy's brow. "What kind of glitch? You're feeling okay, aren't you, Lily?"

The little girl nodded, her pretty blue eyes big and uncertain.

"Not a medical problem." The woman laid a comforting hand on Lily's shoulder. "We've run into a housing problem. Things at Lily's last home didn't work out."

Lily looked away, tugging at the bottom of her shirt. "My foster mom said she was too busy to spend so much time at the hospital. I told her she didn't have to sit with me. That she could just drop me off and pick me up later, but she said she couldn't do that. She said I had to be with a family with more time."

Josie's heart twisted into a hard, aching knot. The tiny girl had to be talking about going to the hospital for her dialysis treatments. She was six years old and she was offering to make those scary, painful trips alone—offering, no doubt, to do anything that would have kept her in that family.

Tears stung the back of Josie's eyes. With her years of being tossed from one house to the next, she had a pretty good idea what Lily was feeling right now. Knew the cold fist that would be squeezing Lily's belly, the anxious fire that would be crawling along her nerves, the aching emptiness that was filling her heart as she wondered if she would ever have a place in the world. Add the fear of a life-threatening disease to that mix…

God.

"Unfortunately," Ms. Turner said, "we're a little short on extra foster families this month, so we're stuck with a bit of a dilemma. I could send Lily to a group home, but I'm worried her hospital appointments might not get the priority they need."

No, they wouldn't. The child-welfare system was overflowing with lost and abandoned children. In an effort to keep up with the massive flow, they maxed out the group homes. And while many of the adults running the group homes had the best intentions, with too many kids to care for, they just couldn't keep up.

"So," Mrs. Turner went on. "I was hoping perhaps you and Mr. McCade might take Lily for a while. Her treatments do take some time, a couple of hours three times a week. But we were hoping you could fit them into your schedule."

"Well…" Crissy looked stunned. She obviously hadn't seen the question coming and was unprepared to give an answer.

"I understand you'll have to speak to your husband first. But I was hoping he might be home, as well, so we could speak to him right away."

Josie remembered the soul-crushing desperation of standing in someone's foyer, hoping—hell, praying— they'd want her. That she wouldn't be turned away— again. There was no more miserable feeling in the world.

She wanted to tell the social worker she'd take the child. But volunteering to take Lily would be ludicrous. She didn't even have a home of her own at the moment.

And with the barn being nothing more than an empty shell waiting to be transformed, she wouldn't have anything that resembled one for quite a while.

And once Crissy got over her shock at being asked to take Lily, she would take the child on, Josie knew she would. And Tate would back her up on the decision. Both Crissy and Tate knew what it was like to face the world alone. They wouldn't let someone as small and defenseless as Lily do it.

But could they give the girl the understanding she needed? Would they be able to make her feel safe and secure and truly wanted for however long she was with them? Or would they make the same well-intentioned, but emotionally crushing mistakes the foster parents in her own past had?

The simple things were always the tellers. They'd buy their own daughter a real Barbie and an imitation one for Josie. Not a big thing, really, she'd always been ecstatic to get any doll. God knew, there were plenty of foster homes where the kids got nothing. But that she got an imitation Barbie while the biological child got a real one was a clear indication that her status was below that of a family member.

Occasionally, of course, there was the reverse of that. The foster parents went out of their way to make sure she got the best of everything. The fanciest Barbie, fixing up her bedroom with all new things, which was just as bad because it made her feel exactly like what she was—a guest in their home.

And what? She thought she could avoid all those pit-falls? Ridiculous. Trying to second-guess someone whose emotions were as mixed-up as any foster kid's were and provide them with just what they needed was impossible on the best of days. And her life was in complete turmoil at the moment.

She needed to spend every possible moment learning her cowgirl skills. At least until the rodeo. And after that she'd be packing up her home in Colorado and moving to Texas. Complete chaos. And *then* she'd be living in a barn where the only amenities would be a bathroom and kitchen for who knew how long. Hardly a stable environment for a kid.

And yet…

It took one look at Lily to know she needed more than a place to stay right now, more than a compassionate couple to make sure she got to her dialysis treatments. She needed more than Crissy and Tate could give her.

She needed a compatriot, someone who'd been there. Someone who could make whatever house she ended up in seem like a home, a home where a small, lost little girl truly belonged.

There was only one person in this room who could come close to doing that.

Josie pushed up from her chair. "I'll take her. She can stay with me."

"Hey, Buckle-boy."

Tommy Ray looked up from the horse he was grooming to find Crissy striding down the barn aisle toward him. He glanced quickly at his watch. "Where's your girlfriend? She was supposed to be here half an hour ago."

"That's why I'm here. To tell you she won't be coming."

"Won't be coming? She's already lost time to her blistered hands. She can't afford to lose any more."

"She's well aware of that. But Lily showed up on our doorstep this morning and Josie snatched her under her wing."

"Lily? The Lily—"

"That's right. *Our* Lily. Apparently, her last foster parents thought taking her to her dialysis treatments was too much work. So the social worker brought her here, hoping Tate and I would take her."

"So why is she with Josie?"

"Because before I could recover from the shock of being asked to take her, Josie said *she'd* take the little girl."

Of course Josie had taken the girl. It was her angel side at work again. Her soft, sweet gentle side. The side that had her talons sunk in him to the bone. She'd know exactly how horrible Lily would feel standing there. No way she'd let Lily go through that.

And poor Lily. He shook his head. "What the hell were her last foster parents thinking? Too busy to take care of a little girl." He'd like to wring their necks.

"Well, Lily's in good hands now. Josie will take care of her, make sure she has what she needs. Which is why she asked me to let you know she won't be working with you today. She's going to spend the day with Lily, get her settled in."

"Got it. But she absolutely needs to be down here tomorrow, bright and early."

"She'll be here, but she can't be dragging Lily out of bed at 5:00 a.m. She needs her rest. Think sevenish. And since you won't be teaching Josie today, I have another chore for you."

"And that would be?"

"I want you to go to the pound, see what dogs they have there."

He raised a brow. "You want a dog?"

"Not particularly, but I don't want you thinking I'm not a woman of my word. You do remember what I said last week, don't you?"

You hurt my girl again, I'll carve your heart out and feed it to the nearest cur.

He ran a hand down his jaw. "Yeah, I remember."

"If what Josie told me about last night means anything, you don't think I'm serious. And since I realized we had no dogs on the ranch last night, I thought I should remedy that."

He gave her a dry look. "And you want me to pick out the dog you're going to feed my heart to."

She gave him a big smile and headed back the way she'd come, talking over her shoulder. "I called the pound before I wandered over. It opens at ten. I want something big. With lots of teeth."

Chapter Nine

"Come on, Lily. You about ready?" Josie leaned in the connecting doorway between her bedroom and Lily's, hurrying Lily up.

"I'm almost ready, I just have to tie my shoe."

Josie smiled at the concentration on Lily's face as tiny fingers worked the thick shoelace. Yesterday afternoon Crissy had suggested that if Josie was going to take Lily under her wing, she might want to move her stuff to the master bedroom since it had a connecting room. It was the perfect idea. Last night Josie had been able to leave the connecting door open, making it possible for Lily to have her own room—a rare and true treat in the foster-care system—and still not feel as though she was completely alone, a fear Josie remembered far too vividly.

Josie nodded toward Lily's shoes. "Those are pretty cool tennies. Lights flash in the heels?"

Smiling, Lily nodded as she pulled the bow tight. "Watch this." She jumped off the bed onto the carpeted floor and danced, her arms and leg moving in typical six-year-old fashion—no rhythm and less grace, but plenty of joy. Pink and blue lights flashed like neurotic fireflies in the heels of her tennies.

Josie chuckled, glad that Lily was settling in well. Of course, the Big T was a help. How could a kid look at all the cows and horses and open space and not consider it their own private Disney World? "Yep, pretty cool tennies."

Lily stopped, pushing a wispy stray curl out of her face. "We're going to see more baby cows today, right? You're gonna rope 'em?"

"Not a real one, remember? I'm practicing on a bale of hay with a plastic head stuck in it."

The child's face fell. "Oh, yeah, I forgot. Can we see the baby cows after?" she asked hopefully.

"I don't see why not." The Big T's Santa Gertrudis babies with their dark red coats, thick necks and cuddly wrinkles had stolen Lily's heart yesterday when Josie had taken her around the ranch.

The sparkle bounced back into Lily's eyes. "Let's go then. Get this roping done." She charged out of the room.

Smiling, Josie headed out through her room, swiping Tommy Ray's hat off the dresser as she went. A twinge of guilt slid through her as she dropped it on her head. There had been a hundred hats at Tott's. She should have picked one out, one that actually fit her, and returned Tommy Ray's.

But none of them had piqued her interest. And none of them had carried the spicy scent of his aftershave. Pitiful. She was supposed to be forgetting Tommy Ray, not reveling in his scent.

Shaking her head, she trotted down the stairs behind Lily, watching blue and pink lights flash, refocusing her concentration on what was important for today. Improving her rodeo skills so she could help the cute kid racing in front of her. And if she drew in a deep breath of spice and musk as she made her way down the stairs, well, she was the only one who had to know.

Tommy Ray was waiting at the corral when they got there. His gaze slid over her, those blue, blue eyes turning sultry, his nostrils flaring slightly.

Heat and a thousand needy tingles shimmied through her. Too bad he was protecting his heart. Too, too bad.

Seeing Lily he swept his hat off in courtly fashion and offered the child an easy smile. "Well, good morning, young lady. You must be Lily. Crissy told me you'd come to stay for a while." He held out his hand. "I'm Tommy Ray."

Lily looked a little surprised at Tommy Ray's fancy

The Silhouette Reader Service™ — Here's how it works:

Accepting your 2 free books and gift places you under no obligation to buy anything. You may keep the books and gift and return the shipping statement marked "cancel." If you do not cancel, about a month later we'll send you 6 additional books and bill you just $4.24 each in the U.S., or $4.99 each in Canada, plus 25¢ shipping & handling per book and applicable taxes if any.* That's the complete price and — compared to cover prices of $4.99 each in the U.S. and $5.99 each in Canada — it's quite a bargain! You may cancel at any time, but if you choose to continue, every month we'll send you 6 more books, which you may either purchase at the discount price or return to us and cancel your subscription.

*Terms and prices subject to change without notice. Sales tax applicable in N.Y. Canadian residents will be charged applicable provincial taxes and GST. Credit or debit balances in a customer's account(s) may be offset by any other outstanding balance owed by or to the customer.

If offer card is missing write to: Silhouette Reader Service, 3010 Walden Ave., P.O. Box 1867, Buffalo NY 14240-1867

NO POSTAGE
NECESSARY
IF MAILED
IN THE
UNITED STATES

BUSINESS REPLY MAIL
FIRST-CLASS MAIL   PERMIT NO. 717-003   BUFFALO, NY

POSTAGE WILL BE PAID BY ADDRESSEE

SILHOUETTE READER SERVICE
3010 WALDEN AVE
PO BOX 1867
BUFFALO NY 14240-9952

GET FREE BOOKS and a FREE GIFT WHEN YOU PLAY THE...

Lucky 7

SLOT MACHINE GAME!

Just scratch off the silver box with a coin. Then check below to see the gifts you get!

YES! I have scratched off the silver box. Please send me the 2 free Silhouette Special Edition® books and gift for which I qualify. I understand I am under no obligation to purchase any books, as explained on the back of this card.

335 SDL D7WT   **235 SDL D7W7**

FIRST NAME   LAST NAME

ADDRESS

APT.#   CITY

STATE/ PROV.   ZIP/POSTAL CODE

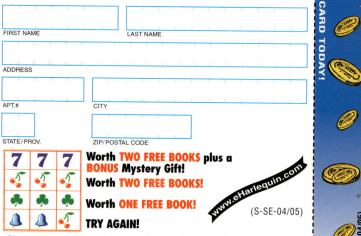

Worth **TWO FREE BOOKS** plus a **BONUS** Mystery Gift!

Worth **TWO FREE BOOKS!**

Worth **ONE FREE BOOK!**

TRY AGAIN!

www.eHarlequin.com

(S-SE-04/05)

DETACH AND MAIL CARD TODAY!

(S-SF-04/05)

greeting, but then, with a giggle she took his hand and shook it. "Hi. You the guy's gonna teach Josie how to rope?" She took another step closer to the cowboy, stretched up on her toes and cupped her hand around her mouth. "She says she's not very good at it." Though whispered, the words carried easily over the Texas air.

Josie smiled.

Tommy Ray chuckled, then he gave Lily a wink. "She just needs a little practice. And some support from her friends."

Lily's brows twisted in thought. "What kind of sport?"

Tommy Ray's lips twitched as he dropped his hat back on his head. "Support. Human support. You know, reminding her it just takes practice, telling her she can do it. That kind of thing."

Lily's expression brightened. "I can do that."

"Good. Let's get started. Twister is ready and waiting."

For the first time Josie noticed the horse tied outside the corral. She gave the horse an apprehensive once-over. "I hope you don't expect me to start roping from the back of that beast today." Lord, she couldn't rope a stationary target while she was standing still, how was she ever going to manage a moving calf from the back of a horse?

"Nope, today we're doing something different."

"Different? But I need to practice roping. You said after two or three days I could start again. And this is day *five*."

"I said we'd talk about it after a few days, but I got a peek at your hands the other night. They didn't look so hot. Let's see how they look this morning."

She rolled her eyes. Did he think she couldn't take care of herself? But she was unwilling to argue in front of Lily, so she held them out.

He took one look and grimaced. "You're definitely not going to be roping for a few more days."

"But I can't afford a few more days. I need every day I have."

He only shrugged. "You have plenty of other skills you need to learn." He pointed to Twister. "We're going to start with riding today. Barrel racing to be exact."

She glanced to the corral. Sure enough, three barrels, set in a giant triangular pattern, stood in the pen. Her nerves drew tight just looking at the barrels. She'd been nervous when she'd started roping because she was afraid if she wasn't good she'd lose the Angels. But there was even more at stake now.

She wanted to make money for Lily.

Yes, Crissy had a bushel of cowboys waiting in the wings to pick up the slack. But *she* wanted to make money for Lily. There was something special about this kid. Something bright and good and precious. She didn't want to disappoint her. She looked back to him. "Okay, barrel racing it is. Where will Lily be the safest?"

"Come here, Lily." He grabbed hold of the child under her arms, lifted her up and carried her over to the metal fence. Sliding her legs through, he set her on one of the middle rails and locked her arms securely over a higher one. "There you go, darlin'. You've got the best seat in the house. Comfy?"

Lily nodded, blond curls bobbing jubilantly. "Can I ride the horse when Josie's done?"

"Not that pony. He's a bit much for a little girl. But we'll work something out, okay?"

Lily nodded, excitement sparkling in her eyes.

Tommy Ray strode toward the horse tied to the rail. As he passed Josie he dropped his voice so only she could hear. "If you'd let me know she was coming I would have had a horse ready for her. Sitting on that fence isn't going to be much fun."

"I didn't know she was coming. My original plan was to leave her with Brax. But for a sick kid, she's pretty energetic. I was afraid she'd drive him crazy. You know how he likes his world organized and quiet."

"Don't worry about it, I'll work something out. In the meantime let's get busy before it gets any hotter. You've done some riding here, right? On some of your past visits?"

"Yep."

"Remember who you rode?" He resumed talking in a normal voice, one Lily could hear, no doubt so she wouldn't feel left out.

She did the same. "Chip. Taggert. Monty, I think."

"That's what I thought. Those guys are good, quiet,

dependable horses. This fella is a different cup of tea. He has a lot more get up and go."

She looked at the horse tied to the rail. He looked pretty much like the other animals. But then, what did she know? "That's good, right? We want him to have more get up and go." She couldn't imagine winning any kind of race with the horses she'd ridden in the past.

He nodded. "And this guy has it by the bucketful. You help him out a little, he'll be in the money."

Josie walked to the front of the horse and held her hand beneath his nose, letting him smell her. "Hey, Twister. Sounds like I'll be riding you at the rodeo, whataya think about that?"

The horse breathed in her scent, then blew it out with an equine snort.

Josie laughed.

So did Lily, her child's laughter tinkling through the air like joyful bells.

Tommy Ray smiled as he unhooked the halter that was keeping the horse tied to the rail and slipped it from Twister's head. "Give her a chance, Buddy. She's the sweetest thing that's ever going to sit on your back." He looked to Josie. "Okay, let's get you up."

She took the reins from Tommy Ray and climbed on board. "Stirrups good?"

She slid her other toe into the wooden cup and tested the stirrups' length. "They seem good."

He looked at the position of her leg and nodded. "They look okay. We might want to adjust them after a few runs, but we'll start there." He swung the corral gate open. "Go on in and walk around, let his muscles warm up, get to know each other a little. I'll be right back."

"Where are you going?"

"To get a ride for Miss Lily." He looked over to the little girl. "You keep an eye on Josie until I get back, make sure she does what she's told." He winked at the kid and then jogged toward the barn.

Lily looked over at Josie, her eyes wide with excitement. "Is he going to get a *horse* I can ride?"

Josie smiled. "Sounds like it to me."

A wide smile stretching her mouth, Lily wiggled on the fence as if the mere thought of riding a horse was too exciting for her to sit still.

Josie smiled. She'd dropped the ball on this one, expecting Lily to sit and watch while she had all the fun. But Tommy Ray had picked it up quickly enough.

Lily pointed at her, mischief sparkling in her eyes. "You're supposed to be walking."

Josie chuckled, Lily was obviously enjoying being in charge. "Yes, I am." She obediently nudged the horse into a walk.

She walked by Lily, marveling at the bright, happy-go-lucky child. The kid had been tossed from one foster home to the next. She was sick, the kind of sick that could kill if someone didn't come along with the right kidney for her soon. And yet, the sprite was the most cheerful munchkin she'd ever met.

The tiny waif had guts—in humbling proportions.

She leaned down and patted Twister's neck, whispering in his ear. "Help me out here, boy, I want to help save that little girl."

She'd only made it around the ring once when Tommy Ray jogged back out of the barn, leading a big, rawboned horse behind him. The horse was dark brown with black socks climbing to his knees and a black mane and tail. He wore no saddle as he trotted easily behind Tommy Ray.

Horse and cowboy stopped beside Lily. "Okay, princess, let's get you up here." Tommy Ray plucked Lily from the fence and deposited her on the horse in one quick, easy move.

Lily giggled with delight. "He's big."

"Yes, he is. You scared up there?"

She shook her head and patted the horse's neck. "He's pretty. What's his name?"

"Connor. And I'm not sure he'd want to be called pretty. Handsome maybe," he teased.

Lily giggled again, shaking her head and patting some more. "I think he's pretty."

Tommy Ray shook his head, looking into Connor's big brown eyes. "I tried, son." He led Lily and horse into the corral.

A huge smile filled Lily's face. "Look, Josie, I'm riding, too."

"Yes, you are. And I must say, you look perfect up there." But she also looked pretty precarious. Her six-year-old legs didn't go very far down the big horse's sides. She glanced anxiously at Tommy Ray.

"Don't worry." He tossed the reins over the horse's head, took a fist full of mane in one hand and effortlessly swung up behind Lily.

The move was smooth, graceful and purely masculine.

Warm little chills raced over Josie's skin. He was so sexy. Sexy and sweet… And unavailable. Shaking her head, she refocused on the task at hand.

"Okay," Tommy Ray said. "Let's see how you handle the general gaits. Give him a little squeeze and jog around the ring a few times."

She shot him a sideways look. "For pity's sake, Bartel. I know how to trot a horse."

"Humor me."

"This is ridiculous." But she nudged the horse into a slow jog.

He watched her trot around the ring from his seat on the bay horse, Lily safely tucked in front of him. "Good. Your seat's not bad and your legs are pretty good. You could stretch your heels down some more, but the legs are steady enough. Keep your hand lower, closer to the horse's neck."

She made an adjustment. "Okay, can we move on now?"

He chuckled. "Yep, let's try the lope. Just put your outside leg back and give him a little nudge. Just a nudge, don't kick him like you probably did Chip and Taggert. A kick will send him off like a rocket."

Just a nudge, huh? Remembering how hard it had been to get the other horses into a canter she was pretty sure she'd need more than a nudge. But she wouldn't boot him the way she had the other horses. Stretching her leg back she half kicked, half nudged.

Twister exploded forward.

Josie fell back as the horse shot forward. She grabbed the horn just before she tumbled off the back of the saddle and pulled back on the reins.

But the rein action was obviously too much, too. Twister threw himself into a sliding halt, pitching her forward over his neck. When the horse finally came to a stop, she was able to right herself in the saddle. Laughter filled her ears. She glanced at Tommy Ray.

Yep, the man was laughing. And Lily was giggling uncontrollably with him.

This cowboy stuff just wasn't getting any better. She made a face. "So glad I could entertain."

Tommy Ray choked back his laughter and ran a hand down his face, doing his best to smooth his face into an inscrutable mask. "Try a lighter nudge."

She shot him a droll look. "Got that part, thanks." Very carefully, she pushed Twister back into a walk and then with a feather touch asked him to lope.

Still a little jazzed from the boot she'd given him last time, he jumped into the three-beat gait with more energy than would probably be normal, but it wasn't such a huge leap she got left behind, and a gentle tug on the rein brought the animal back to a nice slow, comfortable lope.

Tommy Ray watched for a few strides. "That looks good. Once you're comfortable there, I want you to move into a gallop. Just give him a light squeeze with your legs and lean forward. The more you squeeze the faster he'll go, so start easy and escalate."

She started easy, but it didn't take long before the game little horse was racing around the outside of the arena full bore. She laughed as the ground disappeared under Twister's pounding hoofs. There were very few things she loved more in this world than speed. And Twister was giving it to her in spades. *And* they were together now. She could feel the connection.

"Okay, bring him to a walk."

Rocking back, she pulled gently on the reins until the horse was once again walking.

"Okay, you've got that down. Let's give the barrels a shot." Sidling his horse up next to hers, he quickly explained the cloverleaf pattern the barrel racers must run. "Got it?"

She nodded.

"Take this first run slow, or as slow as he'll let you. He's used to being asked to work at top speed, and this guy likes his job. So he'll probably be fighting to go faster. Just use the reins to keep him at a pace you're comfortable with until you get the pattern down. Except for on the home stretch. Let him go there. If you're prepared for his burst of speed I don't think you'll get left behind, and I'd rather he not learn to do anything but run full-out there."

She nodded. "Got it." Giving Lily a wink, she went to work.

The first barrel went well. The second barrel she went way wide on. The third barrel was tighter, but she lost her balance for a bit and had to scramble to stay on board when Twister poured on the speed to race toward the finish line. Still, pretty respectable.

She pulled Twister to a trot and returned to where Tommy Ray and Lily were sitting on Connor. "Now that was fun."

Tommy Ray smiled with her. "Not bad for a first try. Wide on the barrels and a bobble at the end, but you did great on the pattern."

"Wide on the barrels? On all of them? I know the second one was bad, but—"

He shook his head. "You want to be in the money, you have to brush the barrels with your leg—without taking them down."

"Wow. Actually touch the barrels?"

He nodded. "Just like a downhill racer brushes the gates."

"Okay, got it." She looked back to the barrels.

"Keep your speed the same or slower if you need. Concentrate on hugging those barrels."

"Yep." She nudged Twister into a walk, returned to the starting position and began again. She turned quicker after the first barrel, but ended up going wide on the far side. She tried so hard on the second barrel she knocked the blasted thing down. The third barrel she completely misjudged, turning before she even got to the thing.

Giggles filled the air. "You totally missed that barrel," Lily hooted.

Josie's stomach knotted. Her incompetence probably looked pretty danged funny. But it wasn't funny. She wasn't going to make one dime for Lily if she didn't pull things together. Not acceptable. Lily had already been let down too many times by too many people. She didn't want to let the kid down, too.

Despite the knot in her stomach, she forced a teasing smile to her lips. "I did not. We just went around it so fast you didn't see."

"Uh-uh." Lily shook her head, blond curls flying as she looked up at the cowboy sitting behind her. "She did not, did she, Tommy Ray?"

Humor glinted in his eyes. "I would have to agree with Lily on this one."

Josie shot them a mock scowl. "Are you two ganging up on me?"

"Yeah, 'cuz you missed that barrel," Lily said adamantly, pointing to the barrel at the top of the triangle.

"You did," Tommy Ray agreed gravely, a smile tugging at the corners of his lips.

She tipped her head, sending him a frustrated glance over Lily's head.

He sighed and did his best to squelch the smile. "Lighten up, Josie. Take a breath. Your first day again, remember?"

She stopped Twister in front of Connor, those knots in her stomach pulling tighter. "But I'm usually really good on the first day. Why is all this so hard?"

He shrugged. "Maybe because most of the sports you've done have been single-man sports. You against the mountain or the race track or whatever. Rodeoing is a team sport. You and your horse. You and the stock. Quit trying to force things. Take a breath and let it come."

Didn't he know what was at stake here? Didn't he know that cute little girl sitting in front of him was counting on her to help save her life?

"Josie." He locked his gaze on hers. "I know."

He was reading her mind. *He was reading her mind.* He'd made love to her with an intensity she'd never felt from a man before, he was attuned enough to her to read her mind—but he was unavailable. How unfair was that?

It didn't matter how unfair it was. It was. What mattered right now was getting this rodeo stuff right. "Then help me."

"I am helping you. You're just not listening. Take that breath and try again. It's going to get better."

It *had* to get better. Or she was going to disappoint the sweetest kid in the world. Big-time. Turning Twister around, she took that deep breath and tried again.

And again.

And again.

And again.

She went wide, she went short, she knocked the barrels down, she even crashed into one of them. Poor Twister'd had to jump the thing to avoid killing them both.

For Lily, who, thank goodness was oblivious to the consequences, it had turned into a regular gigglefest.

But for Josie, it was the roping fiasco all over again. Defeat crushing her shoulders, she rode over to Tommy Ray.

He ran a hand down his face, his expression as haggard as she felt. "You've got a crappy eye."

"Yep, bad eye," Lily chirped in a cheerful voice.

The knots in Josie's stomach multiplied faster than poor Twister was breathing. She looked at Tommy Ray. "What does that mean?"

"It means you've got a good seat and good hands, but you're having trouble gauging how much distance your horse covers with each stride, so you can't judge the best time to ask him to turn. But it'll get better with practice. But not today. Your horse is spent."

She sighed, tension plucking at every muscle in her body. Nudging Twister into a walk so he could cool down, she reached down and patted his neck. "Sorry, boy. Maybe tomorrow will be better." The poor horse had to be as frustrated as she. He was trying to do his job, and she was goofing him up.

Tommy Ray moved Connor in beside her, Lily still tucked in front of him. "Look, part of being a successful rodeo hound is finding which events you're best at and competing in those. Your eye might not be the best, but you've got a good seat. It might be that the rough events will be your forte."

"Rough events?"

"Bronc and bull riding."

"Yeah?" Hope slid through her. She *had* to find something she was good at. Something she could make money at. "When do we start that?"

"As soon as Crissy gets the rough stock here. Just a couple more days."

"Good."

"Can we trot now, huh?" Tired of the adult talk, Lily glanced up at Tommy Ray. "You said we could trot when Josie was done."

Tommy Ray smiled down at the squirming munchkin. "That's right, I did. Come on." He nudged Connor into an easy jog.

Josie watched them move off. Tommy Ray looked right at home on Connor's bare back, his denim-clad legs hanging quietly down the horse's sides, his sexy butt moving easily with the horse's stride. Lily bounced with Connor's gait, but Tommy Ray kept her centered easily, his free hand wrapped protectively around her middle.

Laughter floated back on the hot Texas air.

Lily was having fun. Good for her. Josie wanted her to have every happy moment she could while she was here.

"I wanna run, I wanna run," Lily crowed.

"Okay, hang on." Tommy Ray bumped the horse into a slow lope.

Peals of high-pitched laughter filled the corral. "Faster, faster," Lily squealed.

Tommy Ray pushed the horse's gait up a notch.

Lily squealed with delight.

They'd made their way around the top part of the pen and were now headed toward her on the opposite side. Lily had her arms thrown wide and her face tipped toward the sky. Man and child were both smiling from ear to ear as the horse loped easily around the ring. The shadows in Tommy Ray's eyes were almost gone. Lily's eyes sparkled like sunshine on water.

Tommy Ray leaned down and whispered something in Lily's ear.

Another laugh rippled through the air.

God, he was good with her. More than good. Great. He'd known the second he'd seen her that she would want to ride, and he'd gone out of his way to make it happen. Now he had her laughing her head off. The man would make a great dad.

Too bad he was depriving his own kid of the joy he was so easily sharing with Lily.

Too bad he was still hiding from the pain Melissa had caused him four years ago.

From what she'd seen so far, he had just about everything she'd ever wanted in a man. He was smart, thoughtful, sexy. Caring. If only she could convince him to give them a chance.

Wait a minute.

Why *couldn't* she convince him? At least try to convince him? He'd told her all he was interested in was a fling. And he'd backed off the moment she'd told him she wanted more. But just because he'd backed off didn't mean she had to.

Convincing him to give them a chance wouldn't be easy. He had his head wrapped around his crazy goal as tightly as any man hanging on to a lacerated heart. Breaking through all that would be tricky. And if she didn't pull it off, it was going to hurt.

But if she won...

Chapter Ten

"You sure there're no little girls like me?"

Josie looked over at Lily as she sped down the highway toward Tommy Ray's. "Crissy said the youngest, Priscilla, is ten. But ten's pretty close."

Lily's lips turned down. "Big kids never want to play with little kids."

No, in the group homes, and quite often the private ones, too, the big kids never did want to play with the little kids. But... "Crissy says it's different out here in ranch country. That playmates are too rare to pass up just because of a slight age difference."

The little girl crossed her arms protectively over her chest and stared out the side window. "We'll see."

"Guess we will." She hoped Crissy was right. There were a lot of fun things for Lily to do on the ranch, but nothing was as fun as a playmate. And Lily deserved a fun day, dang it.

Yesterday, Josie had done her best to entertain Lily while the dialysis machine had cleaned her blood. Lily had been a trouper, even suggesting a couple of times that Josie didn't have to stay the whole time if she was bored or had something important to do. But despite Lily's attempt to keep a stiff upper lip, by the end of the treatment she was tired and cranky. A sure sign that the dialysis had taken its toll. So today, Josie wanted Lily to have a good day. A fun day.

And while Lily played with Priscilla, Josie intended to corner Tommy Ray. Though she'd tried the last couple of days to have a private chat with him, she hadn't been able to pull it off with Lily at her side—or while she tried to master her cowgirl skills. So she'd decided to kill two birds with one stone today. Give Lily a play date and carve out a little alone time with Tommy Ray.

She glanced down at her clothes. She wore a top that showed a good four inches of belly and a pair of jean shorts that left a whole lot more skin bare. They weren't Daisy Duke's, but they'd catch Tommy Ray's eye.

Trepidation raced over her nerves. She could be opening herself up for a big hit. But life was a risk. And she had a deep-down feeling Tommy Ray Bartel was worth it.

"Look. There's the cow mailbox Crissy said to watch

for." Lily pointed toward the windshield and the mailbox with its wooden cutouts of a Texas longhorn looming beyond.

"Yep, I think you're right." She slowed and turned down the dirt drive.

The narrow, hard-packed road went straight back about half a mile before stopping at an old, two-story wooden slatted ranch house. Dust billowed around her car as she made her way to the sad-looking abode.

White paint had been peeling in the hot Texas sun for years, if the amount of raw wood showing from underneath meant anything. And the porch sagged. Bigtime. Josie pulled up in front of the dipping boards and killed the engine.

A big German shepherd came around the side of the house, barking loudly.

Lily leaned back in her seat, her eyes locked on the big dog. "He doesn't look very friendly."

Josie smiled. "His tail's wagging. But you stay in the car until I check him out, okay?"

Lily nodded, her eyes wide as she watched the big, noisy animal. "No problem."

Chuckling, Josie got out of the car.

The dog headed in her direction, its bark getting a little louder.

An uneasy tremor slid down her spine. Maybe she should have followed Lily's lead and stayed in the car.

But before things could get out of hand, a woman stepped out onto the porch. "Buster, that's enough."

The dog immediately quieted and stopped where he was, a good ten feet from Josie.

"Can I help you?" The woman's gray hair gave away her status as the previous generation, but the smile turning her lips was friendly and welcoming.

Mrs. Bartel, Tommy Ray's mama, Josie presumed. "If this is the Bartel place you can."

"This is it. What can I do you for?"

"I'm Josie Quinn, one of the Alpine Angels. Tommy Ray's been helping me learn how to rodeo over at the Big T."

The woman's smile got a little wider. "That's right, he's been telling us all about your progress."

Josie laughed. "Those must have been short conversations."

Gentle humor filled the woman's eyes. "He says you just need to relax, quit trying so hard."

"Yeah, I've heard those words a few hundred times."

"They working?"

Josie sighed. "Not that I've noticed."

Mrs. Bartel chuckled. "Well, bring your little friend and come on in. I'm guessing you're here to see Tommy Ray."

"If he's not too busy." Josie waved Lily out of the car.

"He and his dad and brother are in the garage working on their pet project." She held the screen door open, inviting them in. "In case you haven't guessed, I'm Nancy, Tommy Ray's mother."

Josie shook Mrs. Bartel's hand as she stepped into the house, the smell of baking cookies filling her senses. "It's nice to meet you, Nancy. And this is Lily." She settled her hands on Lily's shoulders.

Nancy closed the screen and held her hand out to the little girl. "Hi, Lily. Tommy Ray tells me you like to ride horses."

Lily shook the offered hand, nodding, blond curls bobbing. "He has to help because the horses are so big. But it's fun riding with him." She stretched up on her toes, just as she had with Tommy Ray the other day, and semiwhispered. "He lets the horse run sometimes. That's my favorite."

Nancy chuckled. "I think that's every little girl's favorite."

While Nancy and Lily talked, Josie glanced around for the source of the telltale video game music, beeps and clicks. Two boys in their midteens were sitting on the sofa, playing. Smiling, Josie took in the rest of her surroundings. Wooden floors stretched in every direction, their soft patina no doubt created by generations of feet polishing them. Braided throw rugs covered large and small areas, giving the place that western, ranchy feel while the big, well-used furniture made everything seem easygoing and cozy.

Crows of triumph erupted from one of the boys on the sofa.

"*Boys,* where are your manners? We have company." Nancy's admonishing tone brought both boys up short.

They dropped their hand controls, pushed up from the sofa and nodded their heads in a synchronized bob. "Ma'am." Their rough male voices echoed in unison.

"Josie, I'd like you to meet our youngest boys, Brach and Tanner." They crossed the living room to shake Josie's hand, moving almost as one.

Josie clasped their hands, envy washing through her. It was so obvious these two moved through life as much as a single entity as they did two independent souls. How many times had she wished growing up that she had a sister who would have offered her that kind of communion?

She hadn't gotten that lucky until she was grown and ran into the Angels.

As soon as the boys had shaken her hand, they headed up an old wooden staircase, arguing about which game they were going to play once they got to their room.

Josie smiled. They may not appreciate their brotherhood, those who had it from birth seldom did, but they were certainly getting the most out of it.

Mrs. Bartel shook her head. "One of these days they'll get civilized. Unfortunately, with boys, they've usually moved out of the house by the time it occurs."

"*Mom,* who's here?" An excited voice sounded over the boys' argument. A little girl, about ten years old, with straight brown hair that brushed her shoulders stood at the top of the stairs. Priscilla, Josie guessed.

Nancy gave Josie a wry look. "The girls aren't much

better." She turned to her daughter. "This is Josie, the young lady your brother is teaching to rodeo, and her friend Lily. If you'd come down the stairs like a polite child, I'd be happy to introduce you."

Priscilla raced down the stairs and came to a bouncing stop in front of Lily. "Hi, I'm Priscilla, but everybody calls me Pris. Wanna come up to my room? We went to a garage sale last week and I got *two* new Barbies." The energetic girl had eyes the same color as Tommy Ray's, bright, bright blue.

Lily's eyes sparkled at the older girl's warm welcome. "Can we play with the Barbies later? Tommy Ray says you have a pony. Can I see him?"

Priscilla looked up at her mom in silent inquiry.

Nancy turned to Josie. "He's safe, and I can send Jen down to watch them. She's fourteen, she'll make sure they don't get hurt."

"Sounds fine to me."

Having gotten the nod, Priscilla ran to the bottom of the stairs. *"Jen, you gotta come with me and Lily."*

Josie tried to hide her smile.

Nancy sighed. "Pris, go *get* your sister."

But Jen was already at the top of the stairs and scowling down at her younger sibling. "Why do I have to go anywhere with you?"

"Because they want to ride Gilly and they need supervision," Nancy said.

"Mo-om, I was—"

"Just going to help your sister."

"That's not fair." But the teen tromped down the stairs, anyway. "Come on, you guys."

The trio disappeared out the back door.

Nancy gave Josie an apologetic smile. "Sorry, it's always a bit of a madhouse here."

"I don't mind." In fact, she liked the noise and the chaos and the undeniable love that permeated the atmosphere. This was the type of home she'd once dreamed of growing up in.

"You want to wander out to the garage or should I fetch Tommy Ray?"

Josie waved away the offer. "Just point me in the right direction."

"Follow the girls out the back door and hang a left. You'll stumble into it."

"Great. It was nice meeting you, Nancy."

"Pleasure meeting you, too. People in these parts were always proud of Crissy's daddy, using the Big T to give cowboys down on their luck a second chance. God knows, we appreciated what he did for Tommy Ray. A lot of us were afraid when Warner passed away that his good works would stop. We were all pleased when his daughter picked up where he left off—and added the Angels charity to the pot. Having you four girls host your charity here makes us all proud."

"Well, we love doing them." She waved a hand toward the back door. "I'm going to head on out to the garage, see if I can find your son. Thanks." She pushed out the back door and hung a left. Male voices drifted to her. She recognized Tommy Ray's, but not the others. Young girls' voices floated on the Texas air, too. Josie looked out back to find a ramshackle barn, a small corral and the three girls gathered around a pretty white pony.

Bouncing on her toes, Lily stood at the pony's head, petting the patient animal's wide forehead. The oldest girl was running a brush over the pony's shaggy white coat. A saddle sat on the corral rail, waiting to be put on. From the look of things Lily would to get to ride all by herself. No wonder she was bouncing on her toes.

Josie shifted her attention back to the garage. The wide, metal door was up, and there he was…Tommy Ray Bartel bending over the fender of an old car.

Her heart stopped. Was there anything sexier than a handsome man dressed in well-worn jeans and a muscleman T-shirt leaning over an old car? Not in her book. A warm ache spread through her. He was so everything she'd ever dreamed of.

"Well, hello. Are you lost?"

Josie snapped her attention to the other fender where an older man and a boy in his late teens stood. It was the older gentlemen who'd spoken, Tommy Ray's dad. She smiled at him. "No, not lost. I came to see your son." She tipped her head toward Tommy Ray.

Tommy Ray looked up from what he was doing, a smudge on his cheek, a wrench in his hand. His gaze slid over her from her bare, sandal-clad toes to her shiny pink lip gloss. Pure male appreciation sparked in his eyes. "Hey."

"Hey, yourself. Gonna introduce me to your family?"

"Absolutely." He looked to his dad. "Daddy, this is Josie Quinn, the Angel I've been working with at the Big T. Josie, my dad Ray."

His dad held out grease-stained hands. "We'll skip the handshake, but I can't tell you how pleased I am to finally meet you. We've been hearing all about your adventures as a cowgirl."

She rolled her eyes. "So your wife said. Can't tell you how glad I am Tommy Ray's been sharing my misery."

The man smiled, wiping his hands on a rag he pulled from his pocket. "It's quiet out here in ranch country, folks tend to share everything. Especially their misery. But you hang in there, you're going to get it." There was nothing but belief in both his tone and expression that she could pull off what she was beginning to think was the impossible.

A different type of warmth slid through her. The kind of warmth that snuggled closely around her heart. "Thanks for the encouragement. I certainly intend to give it my all." Though if the past days' practices meant anything, her all wasn't going to be enough.

"I'm sure you do." He tipped his head toward the teenager. "This is Mark. He's a senior and getting ready to go to Texas A&M. On a full academic scholarship." Pure pride shone in the man's eyes—blue, blue eyes he'd passed to his oldest son and at least one of his daughters.

Josie smiled at the teenager. "Hey, congratulations. Texas A&M. *Very* impressive."

Red crawled up the boy's neck, but his smile was wide. "Thanks. I'm pretty excited about it."

"I'll bet you are."

"So excited he can't talk about anything else these days," the proud father teased. "But we're pretty excited, too, so we let him yammer. Come on Mark, let's head inside for a cold drink." He tipped his head toward Josie. "Nice to meet you, young lady. Hope you stop by again." Without another word he left, Mark at his side.

She looked to Tommy Ray. "Nice guy, your dad."

"The best." There was as much pride in the son's eyes as there had been in the father's.

So Tommy Ray knew how lucky he was.

He grabbed a rag from the fender of the car and started wiping his hands on it. "So, what brings you here?"

"Thought I'd wander over, see what you did when you weren't cowboying." She gave the car they'd been working on a closer look. A Cadillac convertible.

She strolled down the side, running her finger over the paint-stripped body. "An Eldorado Biarritz. 1957. Convertible of course. Nice, cowboy. Very, very nice." At the rear of the car, she lovingly traced the curved, puffy fins that made the '57 Seville and Biarritz unique. "You gotta love the chipmunk cheeks. How long have you been working on her?"

"Daddy and I found her in a backyard about two years ago abused and neglected. But the three of us just about have her ready to rule the roads again. She's re-upholstered and the engine's pretty much where it needs to be. A little more tweaking and I'll have it singing as sweet as a lovebird at dusk."

She chuckled softly. "I'll bet you will." She strolled to the middle of the car, taking in the new upholstery. "White leather, huh? What makes me think if I take a good look, I'll find a couple cans of fire-engine red paint hanging around?"

Smiling, he pointed to a black metal rack where three cans of automotive paint sat. "Mixed and ready to go."

She shot him a cheeky glance. "I'll have to sneak in one night soon, add some white."

He cringed. "Don't even think it."

She tipped a shoulder, still smiling. "We'll see." She ran her finger over the car again, studying the sleek lines, thinking about the three men she'd found working on it. "You're cheating him out of this, you know?"

"Cheating who out of what?"

"Your son. Out of helping you all fix this car."

He scowled at her. "Is that why you came over? To harass me about my son?"

"No. I came over to convince you to give us a

chance. But then I saw you three out here, working on the car. Saw the pride in your dad's eyes when he looked at you two, when he talked about Mark going to college. It just made me think of little Tommy. Of what he's missing."

He'd stilled when she mentioned the part about giving them a chance, but as soon as she moved onto Tommy Dean, his scowl returned. "He's *six*, Josie. You think I'm going to prop him on the fender while he tunes the engine? And I'm working on getting us back together."

"No, you're working on some crazy goal that your son is not going to care about. And there're things a six-year-old could do out here. Hand you wrenches. Pick up the nuts you drop on the floor. Bet your dad had you out here at six."

He looked away, his lips pressed into a thin line.

"That's what I thought."

He looked back to her, his expression hard. "Haven't we been over this?"

"You've run away from this discussion before, yes. And the other night I let you. But I've been giving this subject a lot of thought. There's something between us, Tommy Ray. Something warm and good and…powerful. I know you feel it, too. I see it in your eyes when you look at me, in the way you react to me when we're close. I want to give whatever is between us a chance. A chance to become something real."

Something that looked an awfully lot like longing

flashed in his eyes, but then he blinked and it was gone. "I told you what I had to offer you. That hasn't changed."

"I know what you offered. But, like I said, I want more than a fly-by-night fling." She locked her gaze on his. "And I'm going to fight for more. I know Melissa hurt you. I know you're afraid of being hurt again. But you need to move on."

"I told you, I'm over Melissa. My goal isn't about her, it's about my son."

"Keep telling me, maybe I'll believe it one of these days. But not today. Oh, I believe you think you need that money to be worthy in your son's eyes. Which is damned ridiculous, and something you need to give serious thought to, in my opinion. But, that issue aside, if your only concern was making that money for your boy, you wouldn't have a one-night rule."

"I told you, I need to keep my head in the game."

"And I've given that statement serious thought, too. It just doesn't wash. Come on, a one-night rule? That's too extreme for a man who just wants to make sure no woman thinks he's making promises when he's not. That's a man who's protecting his own heart. Making sure *he* doesn't get attached."

"For crying out loud, you're like a dog with a bone. Hanging on and refusing to let go."

She smiled. "Well, it's a very fine bone. One I'm not giving up without a fight."

He paced away, tossing a hand in frustration. "Fine,

let's say you're right. Let's say I have a poor wounded heart and I just can't face rejection again. Why won't you just let me lick my wounds in peace?"

"Because it's not good for your boy. He needs his dad. And it's not good for me. I think we could have something good together. And it's not good for you. I see the sadness in your eyes, Tommy Ray. The loneliness. I only have to look at you with your family to know you're not the kind of man who's happy alone. You need people in your life. You need a family of your own. You can't stand on the sidelines for the rest of your life. At some point you're going to have risk your heart again."

"Hey, look at me!" A white pony suddenly trotted in front of the garage, Lily waving madly from the animal's back, her smile stretching from one ear to the other. "I'm riding all by myself."

Tommy Ray, no doubt thrilled at the interruption, moved to the door and smiled at Lily's accomplishment. "Yes, you are."

Josie joined him, wishing Lily's timing had been a little better, but unwilling to let this special moment pass. She clapped her hands. "Look at you. Go get 'em, cowgirl."

Lily's face was brighter than the sun as she trotted around the yard, showing off.

Tommy Ray leaned forward, peeking farther out of the garage as if looking for someone.

Seeing him, Jenna gave him an impatient wave. "Don't worry, I'm watching 'em."

"Good. She's new to this."

"Yeah, but she's good at it," Jenna said. "Look, she's barely bouncing."

Josie watched the little sprite on the horse. She chuckled wryly. "Heck, she rides better than I do."

Tommy Ray shot her a sideways glance. "You ride just fine."

"Oh, yeah, that's right, it's just my *eyes* that are bad."

"Stop it, already. The bronc and bull riding are going to be your events. And there are going to be plenty of cowboys, including myself, donating their winnings, too. Lily's going to get her operation."

"I know that. But *I* don't want to let her down. What is she going to think if everybody's making money for her but me? I don't want her to think I'm not trying, that I don't care."

"She isn't going to think that. You took her in, you're the one who's taking care of her. She knows you care."

Josie scraped her fingers through her hair. "I hope she does, but… After so many years of being in the system, after so many years of feeling like you're a guest in someone's home, feeling like you have to watch everything you say, everything you do or you'll get kicked out again, it's hard to believe someone really cares."

He cocked his head, studying her. Finally he said, "You've gotten pretty attached, haven't you?"

That question didn't take much thought. "It was pretty easy to do. She's a remarkable kid."

He cocked his head, studying her. Finally he said, "Remarkable enough to adopt?"

She rocked back at his unexpected words. *"What?"*

"You heard me."

"Yeah, I heard you," she sputtered. "But I couldn't have heard right. I'm a single woman in the middle of *huge* changes, for pity's sake. I just quit my job, and I'm about to move into a *barn*. A barn that's going to remain pretty darn barnlike for a while. Quite a while."

"An adult used to something a little more luxurious might not be overly thrilled about living in an unfinished barn, but I think a kid would like it. Especially if it was the first real home that kid ever had."

He'd lost his mind. "Fine, forget the barn. Does the lack of a job raise any red flags for you? Last time I looked, kids liked to eat."

"You're not going to have an empty pantry are you?"

"No, but—"

"So how much more can it cost to feed a tiny little munchkin like Lily?"

She shook her head. "I don't get this. You think you need a million dollars in your pocket just to see your kid. But it's okay for me to adopt Lily despite the fact I'm not sure I'm even going to *have* an income for the next year or so. I'm trying to get my sculpting business off the ground, remember?"

"You're not penniless. You said you have enough money to live frugally for a year. And Crissy said your sculptures made good money at the last few Angel events. I don't see any reason why they won't do the same for you."

A thousand thoughts and emotions swirled in her head. Did he have a point? Could she offer the little girl a home? A real home?

How could she? She didn't know what a real home was. She sure as heck didn't know anything about being a mom, she'd never had one. And the way things were going there would be no dad to help with the parenting. She shook her head. "Even if you're right about the money issues, Lily needs a *real* family. A *whole* family. One with a mom *and* a dad. Maybe even a brother or sister or two."

He raised a single, sardonic brow. "And what do you think her chances are of getting that?"

She rocked back at the cold reality of his words.

"That's right. Damned slim."

"But I don't know anything about raising kids. I don't know anything about child health or discipline or how to help them succeed in school. And my own personal experiences aren't going to help. I moved so often as a kid, I was a disaster in school. I think most of my teachers passed me just to get me out of their classes. And my advice to her for handling the snotty girls on the playground would be to paste the little brats. That's how I handled it. And when she gets older and starts dating boys?" She waved away the subject. "We don't even want to go there. No, Lily definitely needs someone better prepared to be a mom than me."

He shot her a sardonic look. "For someone who was just preaching about getting off the sidelines a few minutes ago, you're awfully comfortable there yourself."

"This is not the same thing."

"Really? How is it different?"

"It just…is." How could he possibly compare her not wanting to jump into a parental role with his silly one-night rule? They weren't at all the same.

Were they?

She stared at Lily riding the white pony around the yard. Despite her happy smile and energetic way, she was a sick little girl. A very sick little girl. And while the Angels would cover the cost of the transplant, having the money didn't guarantee a kidney would become available.

And it didn't guarantee the operation would be a success. A cold sweat broke out on her skin. Maybe her reluctance to jump into the game wasn't so different, after all. Maybe it was even centered around the same thing that kept Tommy Ray on the sidelines. Protecting her heart.

Chapter Eleven

Josie stood in the doorway between her room and Lily's. It was late, past midnight. Lily was asleep, the night-light by her bed illuminating her features. Her soft curls were spread chaotically on her pillow, her breathing slow and steady. She looked cute and snuggly and heartbreakingly dear.

Tommy Ray had been right earlier today. Lily's chances of getting a real family were damned slim. Heck, damned slim was an optimistic outlook. No one was going to adopt her. Not today or tomorrow or any other day. No one was going to want this precious little girl.

But Josie did.

It was the scariest thought she'd ever had, making a fragile child part of her life. A little girl who might not see her tenth birthday. She'd tried to make herself step back from the idea a hundred times since Tommy Ray had brought it up, but it hadn't done any good. The time for protecting her heart had passed. Lily already had it. Lock, stock and barrel.

She couldn't give the girl a nuclear family or a fancy house, but she did have one thing to offer. Make that two things.

Understanding and…love.

She had a ton of love to give. A lifetime of love she'd saved up because she hadn't had anyone to give it to.

She wanted to wake the kid up, let her in on the secret. But she couldn't. Not yet. Not until she'd gotten a green light from the state. Which might be a ways off. After all, she was a single, unemployed woman. Convincing them she could provide a stable environment for the little mite could be tricky. But she'd convince them—if she had to move heaven and earth.

And she did have a few things going for her. She was part of the Alpine Angels. Lily would never want for medical attention. And Josie could always go back to work as a legal secretary if necessary. Not her choice of jobs. But for Lily, she'd happily do it.

Tears stinging her eyes, she tiptoed quietly into the room. She brushed the hair back from Lily's forehead and softly kissed her cheek. The softest, warmest, most perfect cheek in the world.

* * *

Tommy Ray closed the chute gate on the scruffy-looking horse and strode into the corral.

The broncs had arrived.

So had the bulls, but no way was he starting Josie on a bull. Her confidence in her rodeo abilities was too low at the moment. He needed to bolster her faith in herself, not set her up for a fall.

He looked over at the corral gate as Josie strode in. She was wearing worn jeans that molded to her hips and legs and a T-shirt that clung to her curves and left a small strip of skin bare just above her belt. The cool morning air had her nipples peaking against the white material.

Heat and need pounded through him like a hard summer rain. What he wouldn't give to run his hand under that shirt, warm her chilled skin with his hands. To drag her back to the big house, back to her bedroom where he'd strip those clothes from her and pull her close.

Enough. Another second of those thoughts and he would be too indecent to be standing in public. He gave her a simple nod. "Morning. Where's your sidekick?"

She hooked a thumb over her shoulder toward the big house. "She's tired today, said she didn't feel up to coming. Brax is watching her."

"She okay?"

"Yeah, I think so. She's not running a fever and her color is good. She does dialysis three times a week, normally every other day. But once a week she has two days in between. The social worker said it was normal for her to be a little run down on that second day. Which is today, so I turned on *Sesame Street* and left her with Brax. He promised to holler if anything looked even slightly out of kilter."

She sounded matter of fact, but he could see the worry in her eyes. The kind of worry a parent had for a child. "You give any thought to what I said yesterday?" After their conversation about her adopting Lily she'd pulled inside herself, her attitude somber and pensive. But this morning she was back to her usual cocky self.

She met his gaze head-on. "As a matter of fact, I did. I'll be calling social services this morning as soon as we're done here. See what I need to do to get the ball rolling."

He was thrilled for her—and Lily. "Congratulations. You tell Lily?"

She shook her head. "I don't want to get her hopes up until I get a green light from the state."

"Probably a good idea." He wanted to pull her into his arms, give her a big hug. But he settled for giving her shoulder a squeeze. "I'm proud of you. You and Lily are good for each other. How does it feel, being a prospective mom?"

"It feels pretty danged good. In fact, just about everything in my life feels pretty danged good right now. Amazing considering I was sure my life was falling apart when I first arrived at the Big T."

He remembered. "But you took the bull by the horns, made some big changes."

"Yep. Just one more piece to bring into place."

He cocked a brow in question.

"You, cowboy. You sidelined our discussion pretty neatly yesterday, bringing up the Lily thing. But I'm not letting you off the hook that easy. I went over to your place yesterday to convince you to give us a chance. I haven't changed my mind."

Desire and longing—and flat-out panic—bombarded him. He'd had plenty of time to think over her words. Was he over Melissa? Was he over the pain she'd caused? Was he hiding behind his million-dollar goal? Using it to keep from putting his heart on the line?

Absolutely not.

Although, considering the disaster his first marriage had been, who could blame him if he was?

But he wasn't.

And the way he reacted to Josie proved it. His body leaped into overdrive every time she was within a country mile. More telling was the ache she generated deep inside him. The ache that reminded him of the dreams he'd once had. Dreams of a home with a good, loving woman at his side and a dozen rug rats running around underfoot. Would he be feeling any of those things if he wasn't over Melissa?

No way.

He was over Melissa. Completely. Totally. One hundred and ten percent. It wasn't his fault he had a goal that prevented him from acting on those feelings. Wasn't his fault he needed that money to be accepted in the world his son was being raised in. It was just the way it was. "I haven't changed my mind, either. If you're interested in a short-term, no-strings-attached fling, I'm your man, otherwise…"

She shrugged, totally unfazed. "Not interested in the fling. But I'm not giving up on you, either. I'm going to do everything in my power to make you see the error of your ways."

He steeled himself against the emotions swirling inside him. "It won't do you any good."

"We'll see. On a totally different subject, Lily wants you to come with us to dialysis tomorrow. Says you make her laugh. So I promised I'd ask. Will you come?"

He shouldn't. Josie and Lily were going to be a family now. And the last thing he needed was to get caught up in the whole family thing. He had a family. At least part of one. An ocean away. He needed to concentrate on that. And he didn't want Lily casting him in the dad role when that wasn't ever going to happen. But the thought of her in the hospital with giant needles sticking out of her…

He'd do anything to make that go easier. "Tell her I'll be there." But how he was going to take her mind off the unpleasantness, he didn't know. Last time he'd checked, they didn't let horses into St. Anthony's.

"Good. You want to go together, or do you want to meet us at the hospital?"

A sudden thought occurred to him. He wasn't sure how he'd entertain her at the hospital, but he knew how to make her smile once they got back to the ranch. "I'll meet you there."

"Okay, tomorrow at ten."

"Good enough. Now, today's assignment." He waved a hand toward the chutes—the small pens built onto the side of the corral. "The rough stock arrived late last night, so today you get to ride your first bucking horse."

Her brow furrowed with trepidation. "I don't know whether to be excited or scared."

"Excited. This is going to be your event."

She shot him a skeptical glance.

He leveled his gaze on her. "You're going to be good at it."

"Well, if not, Angel reinforcements should be here anytime."

"What's anytime? Today? Tomorrow?"

"Any minute, actually. Their plane got into Houston late last night. They thought they'd be here by seven, at the latest." She glanced at her watch. "And it's already six-thirty."

"Good. Did they say how their skills are coming along when you talked to them?"

"You'll be happy to know, they're both doing way better at roping and barrel racing than I am."

"Good. Have they—"

"*Good.*" She punched his arm. "That's not nice."

"Of course it is. I want you all to do well."

She gave an indelicate snort.

He smiled. "Don't worry. You're going to kick their butts in the bucking events. Have they been practicing any bareback or bull riding?"

She shook her head. "They're saving that for you."

"Okay. The rough stock is still tired from last night's late arrival, so they won't be up to their usual performance. Perfect for beginners."

"I can hope." She glanced at the two horses already in the chutes.

He followed her gaze. Stomper, the horse on the left was standing as still as a statue, his head hanging to the ground, his eyes closed in his usual, deceptive, couldn't-get-me-to-buck-with-a-cattle-prod pose. Crusher wasn't nearly so subdued. He swung his head, taking in every little detail, the whites of his eyes showing, making him look wild-eyed and unpredictable.

Josie pointed to Stomper. "I think I'll start with the one on the left. Leave Wild Bill there to Mattie and Nell."

He smiled. "Old Stomper it is."

"Stomper?" she squeaked, looking back to the horses. "Maybe I should reconsider Wild Bill."

He chuckled. "If it's the name pushing your decision, you should know that Wild Bill's real name is Crusher."

"Yikes. I'll stick with Stomper. Are you going to give me any words of wisdom or do I just crawl on and pray for the best?"

"Words of wisdom, definitely. First off, Stomper's a good, straight-ahead bucker with no tricks in his pocket. A perfect starting horse for beginners."

Confusion and surprise filled her expression. "Didn't these horses come from a different state?"

"Ten Oaks in Oklahoma."

"Then how do you know what kind of bucker he is?"

"You go to enough rodeos, you get to know most of the rough stock in the country."

She shot him a look. "And we both know how many rodeos you've been to."

He met her gaze head-on. "Yes, we do. Do you want to hear what else I have to say or do you want to just crawl on? See what happens?"

"Oh, I definitely want to hear your words of wisdom. But that doesn't mean I'm not going to share a few wise words of my own. Now go on. Stomper is a good, straight-ahead bucker with no tricks in his pocket. And…"

"And the number-one thing to remember is—hang on tight and lean back as far as you can from the moment the gate swings open. Even if you think you're leaning back, lean back farther. Otherwise you're going to find yourself flying over his head before you know it." He pointed toward the cowboy sitting on the rail above Stomper. "Trent's going to help you get on and give you a few tips about sitting and hanging on to the handle pad. And then the fun begins."

Worry pulled the corners of her mouth tight. "And

what are you going to be doing while Trent's showing me how to do all that?"

"Don't worry, I'm going to be right here. I'm your pick-up man." He pointed toward the saddled horse tied on the rail. No one was plucking her off that horse but him. "Ready?"

She took a deep breath and let it out slowly, staring at Stomper like he was the anti-Christ. "I guess."

He gave her shoulder an encouraging squeeze. "You're going to do great. This is your event."

A car horn sounded in the background.

They both turned to see a blue, midsize sedan zipping down the road, dust billowing in its wake.

He raised a brow. "The two missing Angels, I presume."

"Oh, yeah." Her response was lackluster at best.

He glanced over at her. "You're not happy to see them?"

"I am glad to see 'em." She grimaced. "I was just hoping to have my maiden voyage behind me before they showed up. If I'm going to make an idiot of myself, I'd rather do it with as limited an audience as possible."

"You're *not* going to make an idiot of yourself."

She sighed, watching the blue car pull up to the corral. "Let's hope not."

A tall blonde with a runway model's body and a shorter one with a small delicate body got out of the car and waved enthusiastically. "Hey, Jos, we're finally here."

Josie strode toward the rail the two girls were crawling through. "So I see."

Hugs were exchanged all around.

Tommy Ray sauntered over to join them. Just a few short weeks ago, he would have thought he was in heaven surrounded by three beautiful women. Now, only one interested him.

Josie waved a hand toward him. "Guys, this is Tommy Ray. Tommy Ray, Mattie." She waved a hand toward the tall blonde. "And Nell." She waved toward the petite woman.

He shook hands with both ladies. "Glad to finally have you two here. I hear things are going well in the roping and barrel-racing arenas."

"Well enough." Mattie rubbed her hands in glee. "I can't wait to meet my horse. Crissy says Tailwind is fast, fast, fast."

He smiled. "That he is."

"Speaking of Crissy," Josie said. "You guys going to go to the house and say hi to her?"

Tommy Ray smiled. She was trying to insure a private first ride.

But Mattie shook her head. "Heck no. Looks like too much fun is happening here. I'm sure Crissy heard us honking, anyway. She'll probably be out any minute." She nodded toward the chutes. "Are those the bareback horses? Are you practicing the bucking events?"

"We were just getting ready to," Josie said.

"Cool." Nell turned to Tommy Ray. "Are we going to start that today, too?"

"You two up to it?" he asked.

"Absolutely," the blond duo chorused.

He nodded toward the fence. "Grab a seat then. Once Josie's done, we'll get you up." He turned to Josie. "Ready?"

She wiped her hands down her jeans. "Yep."

He walked with her as she headed for the chutes, lowering his voice so only she would hear. "You're going to do fine. Just—"

"If you tell me to relax, Bartel, I'm going to kill you on the spot."

He chuckled. "Okay, how about a distraction instead? Maybe that'll help you relax. I'm painting the Biarritz this weekend. You and Lily want to go for a ride when she's done? We could take her into town, have an ice-cream cone." More of the family stuff. But he couldn't think of another distraction right now.

Her expression brightened a bit. "Yeah, we absolutely do. But I need a better distraction than that." Her look turned sultry, and to his surprise she leaned in and kissed him, in front of God and everyone.

And it was no quick, chaste kiss. Her body melted against his and her tongue snuck in to tease, entice…promise.

He should pull away. There were four cowboys and two women sitting on the fence hooting and hollering. But he didn't pull away. He leaned in, taking everything she offered. Taking it, reveling in it, savoring it. Man, she felt good.

Finally she pulled her lips from his. Her lips still achingly close to his, she whispered, "Now *that's* a distraction. And a reminder of what you're missing while you hide behind your goal. Give it up, cowboy. And rejoin the living." She turned on her heel and strode toward the chutes, her hips swinging saucily.

The ache that was so often present when she was near squeezed his chest. She was fighting for him. Melissa had never fought for him. Their marriage had been over as soon as her disenchantment with his meager lifestyle had kicked in. He'd tried to hold it together because he'd loved his wife and because he'd loved his son, but he'd been the only one trying. To see Josie fighting for him now, even after he'd told her there was no future for them…

Best not to think about it. He had a goal to achieve. And just because she wanted him now didn't mean she would six months from now. That's about how long Melissa's attraction had lasted.

Doing his best to ignore the fire she'd ignited in his blood, he retrieved his pick-up horse from the rail, mounted and moved to the middle of the pen.

As he watched her lower herself onto Stomper's back he marveled at her tenacity and courage. There weren't many women who crawled on bucking horses, period, and Josie was clearly not comfortable with the idea. But she was doing it, anyway.

He didn't think he'd ever met a woman with such heart.

She snuggled down onto the horse's back, tightened her grip and looked to him.

He gave her an encouraging nod. "Don't try anything fancy this time. Just concentrate on staying on board."

She nodded, tension lining her face. "Got it." She adjusted her hold on the handle pad one last time and gave the cowboy working the gate a nod.

The gate swung open.

Stomper exploded out of it, his front feet hitting the ground as his back feet kicked high. Then he leaped forward, repeating the buck again and again as he cleared the gate and headed into the corral.

Four bucks later, Josie was still on.

Tommy Ray whooped with delight. "Atta girl. Stay back."

She leaned back farther, jerking hard with each buck. But her butt stayed in the middle of the horse's back and her grip stayed tight.

Stomper made his way steadily across the arena, his front feet hitting the ground hard and his back feet reaching for the sun.

Tommy Ray held his breath. Josie was getting tossed around pretty hard. But she was sticking. Good for her.

"That's eight. Pick her up," one of the cowboys hollered from the rail.

She'd done it! Tommy Ray spurred his horse into action, galloped up beside the bucking Stomper and wrapped one arm around Josie's middle. "Let go, I got you." She released her grip and he pulled her from Stomper's back onto the front of his saddle.

She was smiling from ear to ear as she turned to look at him. *"I did it. I did it."* Jubilation bubbled from her words.

"I told you this would be your sport."

Her smile got even bigger. "Yes, you did." She threw her arms around him and hugged him tight.

He should set her on the ground. Let her go. Taking advantage of her excitement just so he could hold her close was a cheap shot. And there were half a dozen bystanders watching.

But his arm didn't let her go. It held her tight. He didn't give a damn who was watching or that he was taking unfair advantage of the moment. He wanted to feel her enthusiasm. Her triumph. Hell, he just wanted to feel *her,* because with their opposing agendas, he wouldn't be feeling her again anytime soon.

"You okay?" Josie looked over to Lily as they drove down the highway on their way back to the Big T.

Lily was slumped down in her seat, her arms crossed over her chest, her face drawn, her small, pale lips turned down in a pout. "I'm mad at Tommy Ray." She kicked at the floor.

"I imagine you are." God knew Josie was going to wring his neck next time she saw him.

He'd never shown up at the hospital. She and Lily had watched for him, waited for him, told each other surely he'd be there any minute. But he'd never come. And Lily, who'd been tired and cranky and none too thrilled to be in the hospital, had felt worse with every passing minute.

"How much longer 'til we get home?" Lily whined. "I want to lie down and watch my movie."

"Soon. We'll be home soon. I'll get you tucked in on the sofa, put the movie on the big screen and make you some popcorn. How does that sound?"

Lily only shrugged as she stared out the window, her expression sad and forlorn.

Josie knew exactly how she was feeling. Unimportant and unwanted. How many times as a kid had she counted on someone to do something with her or for her only to have them blow her off at the last minute? More times than she cared to remember. After all, she was only the foster kid. Most of the families she stayed with thought she should be grateful they'd let her into their homes at all. Expecting them to go out of their way for her had only brought disappointment. It was a reality of life she'd learned to live with.

But seeing Lily grapple with those same dark thoughts… On top of being sick…

Tommy Ray better have a danged good excuse for missing the hospital. Or he was going to be one dead cowboy.

"I 'spose he could have just got busy," Lily said, her words soft, sad. "Forgot about us. I forget sometimes."

Josie's heart squeezed. She was making excuses for the man. "I don't think he forgot, honey." He'd told her just before he'd headed home last night that he'd be at the hospital today. "But he might have been busy. An emergency might have come up." And it better have been a big one.

Lily looked to her. Guilt shaded her eyes, but anger kept her chin tipped up. "I'm mad at him."

Poor kid. She was mad Tommy Ray had ditched her, but her years as the unwanted kid had taught her she had no right to be angry, that she should be grateful Tommy Ray bothered to spend time with her at all.

What bull. If Josie had anything to say about it, she was going to change that attitude—quick. Lily didn't have to settle for whatever someone wanted to throw her way. She had Josie now. "Well, you can be mad at him. I'm mad at him, too." And she intended to tell him so as soon as she got Lily snuggled onto the sofa with her popcorn and movie.

"Come on, Gilly, get your snowy ass out of there." Gritting his teeth, Tommy Ray pulled on the pony's tail, encouraging him to back out of the trailer.

Gilly didn't move.

Tommy Ray glanced at his watch. Almost one. He was late. Way late. He'd undoubtedly missed the dialysis treatment altogether.

Josie and Lily were probably already on their way back to the ranch. He should have remembered how long it had been since Gilly had been in a trailer. Should have remembered what a pill the pony was about getting into one period. But he hadn't remembered—until the obstinate animal had stopped dead the second his foot had hit the loading ramp.

If the beastly animal had been smaller, he'd have just picked him up and shoved him in. But at fourteen hands, Gilly was too big to pick up and put anywhere. And with his youngest sister watching, he hadn't been able to use the most efficient methods of persuasion. The second he'd picked up a whip, Priscilla had put herself in front of the pony as if he was one of Saddam's torturers. For crying out loud, he was only going to tap Gilly with it. But no, Pris wouldn't let the whip anywhere near the pony. So he'd been stuck coaxing the miserable animal into the trailer with carrots.

It had taken almost two hours.

He should have just given up and gone to the hospital. But… Lily'd had so much fun on the pony when she'd visited his folks' place. She'd be thrilled to have the pony at the Big T. And he'd wanted her to have something special. Something to make her forget the needles he was sure were an integral part of dialysis. Once she saw the pony, maybe she'd understand why he hadn't made it to the hospital. At least he hoped she would.

He pulled on the pony's tail again. "Come on, Gilly, *get out*. You obstinate old goat."

Pris, who'd come to make sure her pony was settled

in comfortably—and not tortured by her older brother, crossed her arms over her chest and pinned him with a narrow-eyed stare. "Be nice to him or I'll make you take him home."

"You wouldn't do that to Lily."

"She could always come over to our house to ride him. Then I would get to see her, too. And I wouldn't have to worry about you being mean to Gilly."

"I've never been mean to an animal in my life. I'm not going to start with your pony."

"You could use another carrot to coax him out. It worked to get him in."

He rolled his eyes. "If I feed him any more carrots, he's going to explode." He strode to the front of the trailer, climbed in the emergency exit and pushed the pony back until he was out of the trailer. "There. Now let's get him in a stall." Then he'd head to the hospital, just in case he hadn't missed everything.

As he led Gilly toward the barn, he spotted Josie's car coming around the hills. Damn. Too late. He stopped, waited for them to get closer, then started waving them down.

Spotting him, Josie headed for the barn instead of toward the house.

He strategically placed Gilly in front of him. Hopefully, Lily would understand as soon as she saw the pony that he'd been late because he'd been bringing the pony over. For her.

Josie pulled to a stop next to him. Her window

whirred down. "Where've you been? We thought you were going to join us at the hospital." Her tone was amazingly calm. The anger crackling in her eyes, however, was anything but.

Oh, boy. Big trouble. And understandably so. But right now he was more worried about Lily. He bent down so he could see over to the passenger side of the car.

Lily was hunched down in the seat, the seat belt slashing across her making her look even smaller and more frail than usual. Her features were drawn, no doubt from the stress and discomfort of dialysis, but it was her expression that caught his attention. It was filled with hurt and disappointment.

Damn. "Hey, kiddo. I'm sorry I missed the hospital. I meant to come—"

She made a face that clearly showed she didn't believe him.

"I *did*. But I also wanted you to have a treat when it was all over." He waved a hand toward the pony trying to stick his head in the car. "I thought you'd like to have Gilly at the Big T for a while."

She looked at the pony. Some excitement flashed in her eyes, but not as much as he'd hoped for. And by the time she looked back to him it was pretty much gone. "It would be nice to have him here. But I didn't want Gilly this morning, I wanted you. Just you."

Ouch. "I'm sorry. I thought I could do both. I thought I could load him up, bring him over to the Big T and still have plenty of time to meet you at the hospital. But

Gilly had other plans. It took me forever to convince him to get into the trailer."

"You should have just left him then." Tears welled in her eyes. "I don't like the hospital. I wanted you for a 'straction." One plump tear rolled down her cheek.

Man. He looked to Josie.

She shook her head. "I'm not going to save you. In fact, I'd like to have a word with you." She turned to Lily. "Now that Gilly is here, you feel up to taking him in the barn with Pris?"

Lily made a face, swiping at her tears, but then unbuckled her seat belt. "Yeah, I guess." She got out of the car and made her way around to Pris.

Tommy Ray handed Pris Gilly's lead and watched the girls take the pony away. Lily petted the pony's neck, but her shoulders had a definite slump.

Damn, damn, *damn.*

Josie pushed her door open, got out and slammed it shut behind her.

He held his hands up. "I know. I screwed up. And I'm sorry. *Really* sorry. I had every intention of being at the hospital. But I also wanted to give her a surprise. A surprise that would take her mind off what she'd just been through. I thought—"

"You're not going to excuse your way out of this. Lily was counting on you being at the hospital. She was *counting* on you, dammit. And you let her down."

"I know." He ran a hand down his face, thinking of the tears in Lily's eyes. "I'll make it up to her."

"How? How are you going to make it up to her?"

"I don't know."

She turned away, growling her anger, her hands clenched into fists. When she turned back, her expression was livid. "You are *such* an idiot, you know that? I've worked with slabs of granite that were less dense than you."

"Hey—"

"Don't 'hey' me. When are you going to get it through that thick head of yours that kids don't want grandiose gestures? They just want someone who's *there* for them. Someone to help butter their toast or tie their shoes. Someone who's there to make sure they have a coat when it's cold or enough blankets at night. Someone to make them laugh so they won't think about the *giant needle in their arm.* Those are the things that make them feel loved and secure. Not ponies and million-dollar bank accounts." Turning on her heel, she strode after Pris and Lily.

His gut clenched and a hard ache filled his chest. All he'd wanted to do was make a little girl happy.

Instead he'd made her cry.

Chapter Twelve

The next evening, Josie leaned on the rail of the pen behind the barn, looking at the big, yellow bull in the ring. "Wow, he's quite the handsome fellow, isn't he?"

Standing on the fence next to her, her arms hooked over the top metal rail, Lily smiled. One of her mischievous smiles. "He's *pretty.*"

Josie laughed. The pretty-vs.-handsome thing had become a running joke between Lily and Tommy Ray. And while she wouldn't classify the animal as pretty, he was definitely…something. Something more than handsome. His massive body with its cream-colored coat was impressive. His wide, pointy horns downright intimidating. And the very air around him vi-

brated with personality and power and something…
discordant.

Lily cocked her head, looking at the bull. "His eyes
look kinda funny, don't you think?"

Yes, they did. An uneasy chill chased up Josie's
spine despite the hot evening air.

"Get back from there. That bull's dangerous." The
male voice snapped from behind them.

Josie looked over her shoulder to see Tommy Ray
striding toward them at a hurried clip, the Texas sun a
giant red-orange ball behind him as it headed for the
horizon. Closing the distance between them in a few
long strides, he snatched Lily from the rail. "Josie, get
away from there."

Between the uneasy feeling dancing over her nerves
and Tommy Ray's obvious alarm, she was more than
happy to back up from the pen.

And not a moment too soon. The bull emitted a loud,
angry cry and charged.

They all jumped back as the bull raced toward them,
his hooves pounding the earth.

He hit the rail with a sickening thud and a metal-
lic clang.

They all winced as the animal bounced back, the rail
humming but still solidly intact.

"Ow. That had to hurt." Josie watched the bull snort
at the fence's audacity in stopping him from flattening
his targets. Thank goodness the small corral had prevented him from getting any real speed or power be-

hind his charge. He probably would have broken his neck otherwise.

The animal moved into an agitated pace along the rail, his eyes big and wild—and locked on them.

"Yikes." Josie looked to Tommy Ray. "I see what you mean. That's one mean hombre."

Tommy Ray set Lily down on the ground several feet from the corral, but he kept his hands protectively on her shoulders, making sure she didn't wander too close to the bull's pen.

Josie hooked a thumb toward the snorting animal. "Is this guy one of the reasons Crissy and Tate flew to Oklahoma yesterday?"

He nodded. "The fund-raiser isn't a sanctioned rodeo event. And because it's not, the rough-stock contractor apparently thought he could send some of his second-grade stock—stock he can't send to recognized rodeos. I'm sure he thought Tate and Crissy wouldn't know the difference."

"And my guess is, without you, they wouldn't have."

"No, Tate doesn't rodeo. He wouldn't have reason to know. But I spotted this guy and four horses that don't buck worth spit. I had Crissy call the contractor and demand different animals. Ones I approved of."

Josie stared at the bull pacing in the corral. "That guy can't buck?"

"Oh, no, he can buck. He's one of the most talented bucking bulls out there. In fact, no cowboy has ever ridden him to the bell. But he's a crazy SOB, charges anything that moves. Once he gets a cowboy off, he goes after him. Sanctioned rodeos banned him two years ago. He was sending too many cowboys to the hospital. Which is why we won't be using him. *And,* why he's *behind* the barn. Where nobody is *supposed* to go," he admonished. "What are you two doing back here?"

"Hey, how were we supposed to know he was crazy? No one warned us. And he was crying. We had to see if he was all right."

"He wasn't crying, he was bellowing. And he's fine. He just likes to hear the sound of his own voice. That's why they call him Screaming Jack."

"Yeah? Like Jumping Jack Flash?"

"No, like Jack the Ripper. So don't wander back here any more, okay?"

Josie nodded. "Got it."

He looked down to Lily. "How 'bout you? Understand?"

Lily pulled away from his hands. "I got it." Her tone bordered on belligerent.

Josie knew the girl wasn't angry about being told to stay away from Jack. She was still harboring hurt feelings about Tommy Ray missing her dialysis yesterday. She'd even chosen to stay in the house with Braxton today instead of coming out while Josie practiced her rodeo skills.

Tommy Ray leveled a considering look at Lily. "Still mad at me?" He kept his voice easy, understanding.

Lily crossed her arms over her chest. "Maybe I am."

"Hmm. You gonna stay mad forever? Or let me make it up to you?"

Lily's anger slowly moved toward forgiveness. Finally she said, "I have to go to dialysis again tomorrow."

As olive branches went, Josie thought it was a pretty good one.

Apparently, so did Tommy Ray. He gave his head a single nod. "I'll be there."

A smile flashed on Lily's face, but it quickly gave way to a more serious expression. "You can ride with us this time. That way you won't get sidetracked."

Tommy Ray chuckled and held out his hand. "Done."

Lily shook it, her expression turning downright speculative. "And maybe you could take me for a ride the next day to see the cow babies? You ride your horse and I'll ride Gilly?"

Josie smiled. You had to love a kid who knew when to push her advantage.

Tommy Ray gave his head another nod. "I think that can be arranged."

Lily mimicked the nod, pumping Tommy Ray's hand again. "Good. We'll go right after Josie's lesson."

An animated ringing—*William Tell* Overture—sounded from Josie's back pocket.

Josie froze. She didn't normally carry a cell phone on her. Hers was in her purse in the house. But this was a special phone. One she'd been carrying since she'd become Lily's foster parent. Only one person had the number to this phone. The head surgeon of Lily's transplant team. Its ringing could only mean one thing.

She struggled to get the phone out of her back pocket. No easy feat with her hands shaking so hard. But she finally managed. "Hello." She sounded every bit as anxious as she felt.

Tommy Ray and Lily looked over at her, wondering what was going on.

Josie gave Lily a reassuring smile, tears stinging the back of her eyes as pure joy and flat-out fear exploded inside her.

"Josie, this is Dr. Levin." The friendly, energetic surgeon's voice came in loud and clear through the tiny phone. "You got our girl close at hand?"

Josie reached out, pulled Lily close. "She's standing right in front of me."

"Good." There was a smile in the surgeon's voice. "Her kidney will be landing on the roof in the next hour. Don't pack, just get in your car and get here as soon as you can. Remember, what we talked about. Every minute counts."

"Oh God, I know you told me everything I needed to do when this moment arrived. But I don't remember any—" She burst into tears. Happy, scared, uncontrollable tears. She swiped at them, trying to gain control. "I'm sorry, I just… I don't…"

Tommy Ray stepped closer, concern crumpling his brow.

On the other end of the phone Dr. Levin chuckled,

the sound gentle and soothing. "Just get Lily to the hospital. We'll take it from there. Everything will be fine."

"We're on our way."

"What's wrong?" Tommy Ray asked the second she hung up.

"Nothing's wrong. These are good tears." This was the day they'd been waiting for. The day that would give Lily a chance at a real future. But if the surgery went awry... She shoved the thought aside, it was too ugly to think about. She wasn't going to lose her little girl. Not when she'd just gotten her. And she couldn't let Lily see her fear. She took a deep breath, pulled herself together and looked down at Lily, giving the child what she hoped was an easy smile. "That was Dr. Levin."

Lily's expression brightened, her big blue eyes twinkling. "They have a kidney for me?"

"Yep. Wanna go get it?"

Lily started bouncing on her toes. "No more dialysis?"

"No more dialysis."

She whooped, dancing away from Josie. "Let's go."

Oh, for the bliss of a six-year-old. Josie looked to Tommy Ray. Everything she felt was reflected in his eyes. Excitement. Fear. Hope. He held out his hand to her. "Come on, let's go get that kidney."

"This is ridiculous. The Alpine Angels are holding a fund-raiser for this. Flyers are up all over town. The rodeo is this weekend, for pity's sake. Three days away!

You're going to get your money." Josie paced frantically in the small admissions office.

There was a glitch.

A big glitch. But at least the nurses had whisked Lily off immediately to prep her for surgery so she didn't have to hear any of this.

Tommy Ray was still with Josie, standing like a sentinel in front of the door while Josie argued with the woman behind the desk.

Mrs. Trask, her gray hair pulled into a tight bun, her masculine features set in a closed, professional mask, didn't look the least bit fazed by Josie's words. "I know your plan was to pay for the operation with money from the fund-raiser, but the money isn't in the bank. The hospital needs financial assurance that the bill will be paid."

"I told you, *I'll* be responsible for the bill if by some remote chance something goes wrong with the rodeo."

"Yes, but you also told me you don't have the funds for the procedure. And you're unemployed, correct?"

Josie gritted her teeth. "Yes, but—"

"It won't do, Ms. Quinn. Because of the cost of transplants, the hospital needs more than a promise that a bill will be paid. We need proof it *can* be paid."

Desperation boiled inside her. "Then let me sign the paper stating the Angels charity will cover the bill whether the rodeo is successful or not." Crissy wouldn't have a problem with Josie signing the papers. In fact, it's what Crissy would want Josie to do.

"The only one who can sign that paper is the person

who holds *legal* authority for the Charity. That's Crissy McCade."

"But Crissy isn't *here.*" Despite her efforts to keep it out, her desperation flooded her words. "She's in Oklahoma. And *I'm* one of the Angels. My word is as good as Crissy's."

"I'm sure it is, Ms. Quinn. But the hospital can't accept verbal promises for payment, and your signature isn't legal." The woman's voice made it clear that as far as she was concerned the discussion was over.

Josie felt as if she was going to explode. Her heart was racing, her palms were sweating and her skin felt as though it was about to split open. For the first time, she understood what Crissy had felt as a kid, watching MS slowly destroy her mother and not being able to help. God. No wonder Crissy had started the Angels.

But the Angels weren't going to save Lily. Not if this woman had anything to say about it. There was only one thing left to do. She turned to Mrs. Trask—and started begging. "Lily *needs* this kidney. And if she doesn't get it, there's no guarantee another one will come along in time to save her. Without this kidney she could *die.* There has to be *something* we can do. And I'll do *anything.* I'll work for the hospital until the bill's paid off. I'll—"

"I'm sorry." The older woman just shook her head. "I wish there was something we could do, but—"

The door suddenly pushed open.

Tommy Ray did a quick sidestep to keep from being hit.

Already dressed in his blue scrubs, Dr. Levin poked his head in the door. "The kidney's here and I'm ready to scrub, but the okay hasn't come down from this office. Can't you hurry things along, Mrs. Trask?"

"I'm afraid there's a problem with the financing," Mrs. Trask said.

Concern flashed over the doctor's face. "What kind of problem?"

"The fund-raiser isn't until this weekend," Josie said, praying the doctor might have a solution this woman had overlooked. "And I don't personally have the money for the operation."

The surgeon looked to Mrs. Trask. "I thought we worked that out earlier. Didn't legal work up a promissory note for the Angels charity to sign?"

Josie's stomach turned. If this was his only solution they were in big trouble. "They did, but the only one who can sign it is Crissy. And she's out of the state."

His expression turned grim. "I'm sorry, but if you can't work something out, I need to call back the helicopter that brought the kidney. Get the organ to the next recipient."

Oh, God. She couldn't let that happen. She couldn't. But she didn't know how she was going to stop it.

"I'll pay." Tommy Ray's voice sounded in the small office.

They all looked to him.

"I'll pay," he repeated, looking at Josie. "Don't worry. Lily's going to get that kidney."

Relief poured through her. She hadn't thought of all the money he'd been saving to see his son. "You'll get it back. I promise. Right after the rodeo. Even if I have to make every penny myself."

Smiling, he gave her shoulder a comforting squeeze. "I'd give it to Lily even if I never would get it back. I want to see Tommy Dean more than anything else in this world. But he's safe and healthy. Lily isn't." He turned to Mrs. Trask. "What do we need to do to make this happen?"

"We'll need proof you can pay," Mrs. Trask said.

He pointed to the phone on her desk. "May I?"

The gray-haired woman turned it around so he could dial.

He crossed the room, punched in his number and waited. Finally he started talking. "Brax, this is Tommy Ray. We've run into a problem at the hospital. They won't perform Lily's transplant until they have proof someone can pay for it. I need you to give this woman any of the financial information she needs from my portfolio." He held out the phone to Mrs. Trask.

Braxton, the Big T's bookkeeper and financial advisor, was also a wizard with the stock market. Several of the cowboys at the ranch used his services.

While Mrs. Trask talked to Brax and wrote numbers, Tommy Ray returned to Josie. Taking her hand, he gave it another squeeze. "Hang in there, everything's going to be fine."

Mrs. Trask hung up, made two other quick calls and turned to Dr. Levin. "You've got your go-ahead."

The surgeon gave Josie a reassuring smile. "I'll see you after the surgery. And Lily's asking for you, you should get up there as quickly as you can."

She nodded and he disappeared out the door, his stride long and fast. She turned to Mrs. Trask. "How much longer will this take?"

"Not long. I've got forms for you both to sign and then you can be on your way."

Good. She wanted to be with Lily. As happy as Lily had been about getting her new kidney, she had to be scared, too. Especially now that she was actually at the hospital with nurses she didn't know getting her ready for the big event. Of course being raised in the system, Lily was used to strangers doing things for her. But Josie wanted this time to be different. She wanted Lily to feel as if someone was in her corner this time.

Mrs. Trask pulled some papers from a file cabinet and set them out for Josie and Tommy Ray to sign.

They dropped into chairs and went to work. Josie finished up the consent forms and watched Tommy Ray finish the financial forms, gratitude and respect and something much more powerful bringing the sting of tears to her eyes. She didn't know many people who would sign over their fortune to a child who wasn't their own.

True, he'd probably get the money back, but there was no guarantee. There was always the possibility something could go wrong. And that possibility, slim though it was, would stop most people from signing those papers. But not Tommy Ray. He was signing. As quickly as he could. Pretty hard not to love a man with that kind of heart.

She stilled.

Love?

No, she didn't mean that in a literal sense. Just in a... The protest died an amazingly sudden death. Her heart fluttered, warmed, swelled. She did mean it. In the most literal sense. Clear down to her toes.

She loved him.

Her world tilted. Her stomach did a nervous jig. Had she just fallen in love with a man dead set against committing his heart again?

Tommy Ray strode beside Josie as they made their way to Lily's room, praying everything would go smoothly. Praying Lily would get her new kidney and a new lease on life.

The halls were quiet, the only sound his and Josie's hurried footsteps. It was approaching nine o'clock and most of the people who'd come to visit had already gone home. And nothing was going on in the surgical wing this late. Except Lily's transplant.

"There." Josie pointed to a sign with a big arrow indicating the way to the surgery ward.

They both hooked a sharp right and picked up the pace. He glanced over at Josie; her nerves were drawn tighter than a bow's string. And why shouldn't they be? The kid she loved was about to undergo a life-threatening operation. Hell, his own nerves were stretched tight. But he needed to stay cool. Make sure Josie and Lily had the support they needed. "She's going to be fine, Josie."

"I know." Fear flashed across her face and she closed her eyes. "God, I hope I know."

He laid his hand on the small of her back, letting her know he was there. That she wasn't alone. "No negative thoughts now. Just forward, positive thinking."

She nodded, but he wasn't at all sure she heard him. Her expression was distracted and worried. She licked her lips, her gaze sliding to his. "I haven't told her I'm trying to adopt her."

"I know. You wanted to wait until you knew they'd accept your application. Which makes perfect sense."

Cold fear filled her eyes. "What if she doesn't make it?"

He couldn't let that thought into his head. He'd already lost one child. And while Lily wasn't his, right now it felt as though she was. "She's going to make it," he repeated, determined it would be so.

"She *is* going to make it," she repeated, with the same determination he'd used. But then her resolve faltered. Tears filled her eyes. "But…what if she doesn't? She'll never know someone wanted her."

The reality of her words sank into his bones. "You're right. You're absolutely right. You have to tell her."

She shook her head, panic filling her expression. "But I can't. What if the state won't approve me as a parent? Then I'll have gotten her hopes up, and they'll be crushed."

She was fast approaching meltdown. He stopped, bringing her to a halt with him. "*If* they don't approve you, she will be disappointed. But she'll know you want her. Even if the adoption doesn't work out."

She took a deep breath, trying to pull her emotions and thoughts together. Finally she nodded. "You're right. I'm going to tell her."

"Good. Because I think we're there." He nodded toward the open door ahead.

She swiped at her cheeks. "Oh, man, I can't go in there like this, with tears running down my face. She'll think she's going to die."

He smiled. "No, she won't. She'll know you're happy for her. That is what most of these are about, aren't they?" He gently wiped a wet streak from her cheek.

She managed a wry chuckle. "You tell me. I've never had so many emotions bombarding me at once. I'm happy. I'm scared. I'm thrilled. I'm terrified."

He let out a commiserating sigh. "I know what you mean. But you're going to get through this. *She's* going to get through it. Now, come on, let's get in there before she thinks you've abandoned her."

She drew another deep breath, straightened her shoulders and gave a nod.

They found Lily on a gurney. She was wearing a printed hospital gown, and there was a cap over her head. A single IV was attached to her arm. She looked small and vulnerable, but her expression brightened when she saw them.

The nurse with her gave them an easy nod. "I'll leave you with her for a few minutes. Just be sure she doesn't bother her IV."

"No problem," Tommy Ray assured.

Josie beelined for the bed and took Lily's hand. "Hey, kiddo. How ya doing?"

"The nurse said I could have a Beanie Baby if I was good about the needle." Lily nodded toward her arm where the IV needle was inserted.

"A Beanie Baby, huh? That sounds pretty cool."

"She said she has a cow one."

Tommy Ray chuckled. "You can't ask for more than that."

Lily looked up at him, uncertainty in her big blue eyes. "Are we still going for our ride? When I get out of the hospital? I don't want the babies to get too big before I see them again." She cupped her hand around her mouth, whispering. "They're not nearly as cute when they're big."

He had to laugh. "No, they're not. And we're absolutely still going for our ride. As soon as the doc says it's okay."

"Good. I can show the real cow babies my Beanie."

"Yes you can."

A nurse poked her head inside the room. "We'll be coming for her in about two minutes."

Lily looked to Josie, worry beginning to crease her brow. "You'll be here when I get out?"

"You bet I will. As a matter of fact." She looked over to Tommy Ray, swallowing hard.

He gave her a small, encouraging nod.

She turned back to Lily, a tremulous smile on her lips. "As a matter of fact, if everything goes the way I want it, I'm going to be around forever."

Lily's expression turned quizzical. "What does that mean?"

Josie chuckled, tears popping up in her eyes. "It means I want to adopt you. That is, if you'd like to come live with me. Be my little girl." More tears filled her eyes.

Tommy Ray put his hand on her back again and rubbed, letting her know she was doing just fine.

Surprise lit Lily's face, and the biggest smile he'd ever seen stretched her lips from one ear to the other. "You want to be my mom?" Despite the joy shining in her eyes, her words were whisper-soft and held as much disbelief as happiness.

His heart ached. Lily was only six, but she already knew more about disappointment than she did triumph.

Josie nodded. "Yeah, how do you feel about that?"

"I want to be your little girl," she whispered, as if saying the words too loudly would let someone hear and her request would be denied.

"I want that, too. Very, very much."

Lily reached up and touched one of the tears tracking down Josie's face. "Happy tears?"

"The happiest," Josie said in a watery voice. And then there were no more words. Josie hugged the little girl, and Lily's little arms went around Josie's neck in a fierce bear hug.

Tommy Ray's eyes misted, and he had to blink back the extra moisture. They were two lucky, lucky girls. They were going to be a family.

Two nurses strode into the room. One of them stepped up to Lily's bed with a cheery smile on her face. "Okay, you two, break it up. Plenty of time for that later. Right now, Dr. Levin's waiting for you."

Lily and Josie pulled apart and the nurses started wheeling the bed out of the room.

Lily waved at Josie. "See you later, Mom."

Tears sprang up anew in Josie's eyes, but a smile turned her lips as she waved back. "See you later, sweetie. I'll be the first person you see when you wake up."

The nurses, the bed and one fragile little girl disappeared around the corner.

Josie turned to Tommy Ray. "Oh, God. Did you hear that? Mom." More tears burst forth.

"I heard. It sounded just right to me."

Chapter Thirteen

The next evening Josie carefully tucked the covers around Lily, leaned down and kissed her cheek. "Sleep well, pretty baby. I'll see you as soon as you wake up." Lily had been given a mild sedative half an hour ago and was already asleep, but still, Josie felt compelled to keep the connection between her and Lily active. They'd both been alone for a long time and they had a lot of bonding to catch up on.

The operation had been a smashing success. According to Dr. Levin, the kidney had pinkened up the second it was attached and had gone right to work. Now, almost twenty hours later, hope shone on the horizon like the brightest of beacons.

A nurse walked in, smoothing lotion onto her hands. "How's she doing?"

"Sleeping like a baby," Tommy Ray said from one of the chairs pulled up beside Lily's bed.

Her tread silent on the linoleum floors, the nurse moved to the bed, checked Lily's pulse and held a hand to her brow. "Everything's looking good. You two should go home. Get some rest."

Josie shook her head. "I want to stay. Just in case she wakes up in the middle of the night."

"She's not going to wake up until morning. The sedative will make sure of that. Her body's been through a big event, it needs to rest. So does yours. You're not going to be any use to her if you're sick. And she's going to need a lot of care for a while. Go home, get some sleep while you can. We'll call you if there's so much as a hint of trouble." With those final words, the nurse slipped silently out of the room.

"She's probably right." Tommy Ray stood and joined her at the bed's side. "Not only do you need to be healthy for Lily, but the rodeo's day after tomorrow. If you're not rested, you're going to get hurt. Unless you're not going to participate. Everyone would understand if you'd rather be at the hospital."

She shook her head. "I'm going to participate. I want Lily to know I'm competing for her."

"Then you should get some sleep. It's already ten. Bedtime even under normal circumstances."

She sighed, adjusting the blankets around Lily for

the thousandth time. "I'm not sure I could sleep even if I tried."

"That's because your brain's still buzzing. But the ride home will help relax you. And once you're in bed, exhaustion will take over. Then you can be rested and fresh for Lily tomorrow, instead of worn-out and tired."

She chuckled softly. "Is that how I look, tired and worn-out?"

"*No*. Actually…" His expression softened, and he tucked a stray strand of her hair behind her ear. "You've never looked more beautiful. Motherhood becomes you. But it's been a long day."

She drew a deep breath and slowly let it out. A little sleep would probably be the smart thing. And she was keeping more than herself up here. "Okay, let's go. You need to be fresh for the rodeo, too." She kissed Lily once more and soaked in one more look at her precious face. Then she went to collect her purse from the corner she'd tossed it into earlier.

When she turned back she found Tommy Ray nestling the small cow the nurse had given Lily after surgery and the cowgirl bear Tommy Ray had picked up in the gift shop into the bed beside the sleeping urchin. Josie's heart ached, the love she'd discovered so recently expanding for the thousandth time in the last twenty-four hours. He was *so* good with Lily.

From the moment the child woke from her surgery, disoriented and in pain, he'd been there, doing everything he could to cheer her up and distract her. He'd read to her from a book Josie had bought in the gift shop. He'd presented puppet shows with the cow and cowgirl. He'd even let Lily paint his nails with the sparkly nail polish Josie had bought along with the book. Sparkly *pink* nail polish.

He loved that little girl—as much as Josie did.

And considering the way he'd taken care of Josie—making sure she had coffee, giving her pep talks to keep her spirits up, holding her during the scariest hours—she suspected he might just love her, too. But getting him to acknowledge or act on those feelings… Not so easy. He was hell-bent on keeping an emotional barrier between them.

And how was she going to get by that?

God knew. She was going to have to apply herself to find an answer. Soon. But right now they needed to head home, so she could catch some sleep and be back bright and early in the morning. She walked over, put her hand on his shoulder. "Ready?"

"Yep." He finished tucking in the cowgirl bear and adjusted the covers under Lily's chin, the nail polish winking in the light.

She chuckled. "If you come in when we get to the ranch I've got some nail-polish remover you can use."

He sighed. "Lily made me promise not to take it off. She said it looked *pretty*."

She laughed. "The cowboys are going to give you a hard time."

He made a face. "Not for long they won't. And if Lily wants me to leave it on, I'm leaving it on."

She wrapped her arms around one of his. "You're a good man, Tommy Ray."

He snorted as they headed out of the room. "Just a sucker for little girls."

She chuckled. "That, too."

The ride home was fairly quiet and quick, and before she knew it, they were sitting in front of the big house. She stared through the night at the big, dark windows lining the front. She turned to Tommy Ray. "Come in with me. I can't face an empty house. And I'm not ready for bed yet." She'd thought she'd start to wind down on the ride home, but she hadn't.

Indecision warred on his face.

"Come on, I'm too wired to sleep—and so are you. We could both use a little wind-down time. Come in, I'll fix us a drink." She didn't want him to go. She didn't want to be alone. Not tonight.

He ran a hand down his face, the soft scratch of day-old stubble filling the truck. "Believe it or not, I don't drink."

"Really? You were pretty deep in your cups the night I met you."

"Yeah, well, it's a once-a-year thing. You met me on the anniversary of the night Melissa left with Tommy Dean. So every year on that date, I get drunk. Try to forget it all over again."

The last thing she wanted to think about was

Melissa. "Well, I have soda in the house. Come in, I'll pour you one." She got out of the car, praying he'd follow. Her ears strained for the sound of the truck door opening as she headed for the house.

Finally the creak of metal sounded in the night.

Yes. She stepped onto the porch, glancing over her shoulder. "You want a cola or something with no caffeine?"

He stepped onto the porch with her. "Oh, no. Caffeine is good. In fact, one of those drinks with enough caffeine to make an entire high-school student body crazy would be good. Got one of those?"

She chuckled, pushing into the house. "I'll see what I can do."

Five minutes later she carried two glasses filled with ice and a murky, yellowish-green liquid that she would have been so much better off leaving in its can. She strolled over to where Tommy Ray was sitting on one of the living room's many sofas, his feet stretched out to the coffee table, his hands folded over his stomach. She handed him his drink and held her glass up for a toast. "To Lily."

He clinked her glass and took a sip. "Hear, hear."

She dropped down next to him. Close enough to feel his heat soaking into her. She needed to be close to him. Needed to feel his strength and support.

She dropped her head onto the sofa back and stared at the ceiling, the day's events running over and over in her head. She smiled. "You'd better get out to those pastures tomorrow, talk to those baby cows, let them know they better not do any growing before Lily gets back out there. She's going to be pretty disappointed if they're half-grown the next time she sees them."

He laughed, a low, easy sound. "Yeah, that could be a problem, especially since the doc said it would be a good month before she could go riding. I could take her out in the truck, though."

"Not until she heals quite a bit. I've been in a truck on the ranch's roads. It's a bumpy ride."

"Then I'll bring a couple of the babies and their mamas to the yard corrals. That way Lily can see them as soon as she comes home. Our ride will have to wait until she's feeling better."

"Good idea. She'll love having the calves in her front yard." And Josie loved the way he took care of Lily. Loved the way he always went out of his way to make sure she was happy.

She loved him, period.

And just what was she going to do about that?

The possibility of losing Lily over the last thirty-six hours had shown her just how tenuous life could be, had reminded her with brutal clarity that one had to take every minute and make it count, because there was no guarantee there'd be any others. So why was she sitting down here on the couch making small talk when where she wanted to be was in his arms?

She needed to take action. Now. She needed to open herself up, lay her heart on the line. Scary, but the only chance she had at winning the day. Drawing a deep fortifying breath, she turned to him and said, "I want you to stay tonight."

"Don't worry. I'll stay as long you like. As long as you need to talk."

She shook her head, setting her glass down. "I don't want to talk. I want to go up to my room." She locked her gaze on his. "And I want you to go with me."

He stilled, the air around them becoming supercharged. "No, you don't. You want more than I have to offer, remember?"

"I'm not asking for anything beyond tonight, Tommy Ray. Just give us tonight." She kissed him then, a soft, inviting kiss.

He froze, his breath catching in his throat.

She couldn't let him back away. "Please. I need you." She kissed him again, her lips playing over his, enticing, entreating.

A shudder ran through him. But he didn't kiss her back.

He had the resolve of a bloody saint. But she wasn't going to let him win this round. She had to show him they belonged together. That she could mend his broken heart. "Kiss me, cowboy. The last thirty-six hours have been long and scary, and we aren't out of the woods yet. I need you." And he needed her, dang it. Why couldn't he see that? She ran her tongue over his bottom lip, coaxing.

His resolve crumpled. His lips captured hers.

Yes! She opened her mouth to his probing tongue, giving him free rein, encouraging him to take. Encouraging him to find whatever he needed…in her.

His mouth devoured hers. He pulled her tight, as if he'd pull her into his very being.

She could feel the same raw emotions in him she felt in herself: The helplessness she'd felt as she'd stood by while Lily's life was in someone else's hands. The hours of agony as they'd paced outside the operating room, waiting to see if life would deliver a crushing blow or a stunning victory. The almost painful triumph she'd felt when the little girl—her little girl—had emerged from surgery with her new kidney and a new lease on life.

Now, she wanted to give them all a new lease on life. She wanted to give them all the family they deserved. The family she'd always dreamed of. She kissed him long and deep.

His hand moved to her breast, kneading gently, his fingertips brushing over her nipple.

She moaned, wanting to feel his hand on her bare skin. Wanting to explore his body without the barrier of clothes. She pulled her lips from his, her breathing hard and fast as she pushed up from the sofa, bringing him with her. "Not down here." She quickly led him upstairs. She didn't want to give him too much time to realize what they were doing and run.

As soon as she pulled him into the big master bedroom, she slid back into his arms, picking up where they'd left off, her lips savoring his. She measured the breadth of his shoulders with her hands, the work-sculpted muscles of his chest. He felt so damned good. Hard and hot and so-o-o male. She moved ever downward, enjoying every inch of him until she cupped his long, hard length.

His hips thrust forward, a low growl rumbling in his throat, his hand convulsing around her breast. "Way too many clothes here."

"I'll second that." Her voice was as shaky as her hands as she leaned back and went to work on his clothes, yanking his shirttail out of his jeans and pulling at his buttons.

He followed suit. In record time, their clothes were lying in a heap on the ground. They fell onto the king-size bed together.

His lips recaptured hers, his tongue diving in, establishing supremacy.

She chuckled softly, letting him have his way for a couple of heart-thumping minutes, but then she pulled her lips from his. "You were in charge last time. This time, it's my turn." She pushed at his shoulders and bucked gently beneath him, rolling him over so she was on top.

He settled his hands on her waist, keeping their hips snuggled tight, the sexy smile she'd fallen in love with turning his lips. "Is that right?"

"Absolutely." A quick roll in the sack would go a long way toward taking the edge off. But she didn't want to hurry. She wanted to take her sweet time. Make sure he got her message.

She loved him.

They belonged together.

He could trust her with his heart.

She kissed his chin. "I appreciated you being at the hospital with me today. You were a great help."

"Not a problem. I wanted to be there." His voice was rough with desire as his hands slid down to cup her bottom.

Hot tingles raced over her nerves. "I know you did. But I want you to know I appreciated it. That I appreciate you." She kissed her way down his neck, letting her body glide over his, teasing him, reveling in the feel of him.

His sex flexed against her. A soft hiss whispered through his teeth.

She gave him a wicked smile. "Actually, there's a lot I appreciate about you." She rocked her hips against his. "You gotta love an enthusiastic man."

His fingers bit into her buttocks, rocking her against him. "Yeah? Planning on making this enthusiastic man happy anytime soon?"

"Oh, I plan on making you a very happy man." She nipped at the juncture between shoulder and neck, wondering how long *she* could hold out. She wanted to feel him wrapped around her. Feel him deep inside her. But she also wanted a future with him. And that wouldn't come so easily.

She salved the place she'd nipped with her tongue, tasting him, teasing him. He tasted salty and male and erotic as hell. "I like the way you taste, cowboy. And I like the way you pitch in to help those around you. Volunteering to teach us Angels how to rodeo. Volunteering to participate in the rodeo, donating your winnings. Helping me with Lily. You're a stand-up guy, Tommy Ray Bartel, in a world where there are damned few stand-up guys left."

There was a flash in his eyes that made her think he liked hearing her words, that her praise meant something to him. But right alongside that flash was something else. Something that made her think he was uncomfortable with the compliment. And why not? After all, Melissa had convinced him he wasn't worthy. That the only thing that would make him worthy was wealth.

Crazy. Money didn't make the man. His heart did. And no one had a better heart than Tommy Ray. No one.

She wiggled her hips, and chuckled seductively. "A real stand-up guy. In more ways than one."

"Yeah, well, let's concentrate on the important one." He moved her hips over his again, his hard length stroking the most sensitive part of her.

She sucked in a sharp breath, her fingers gripping his shoulders. "You're killing me, cowboy."

"Then stop talking and take care of the problem."

"Hey, a man should know when he's appreciated. And *why* he's appreciated. Did I mention I like the way you help take care of your family? The way you love them? Not everyone appreciates their family the way you do."

She suddenly found herself on her back, staring up at the ceiling, Tommy Ray once again stretched over her.

He stared down at her, his expression drawn tight with passion. "If you wanted to talk, we should have stayed down on the sofa. You want to go back down there?"

Absolutely not. She shook her head.

"Me, neither." His lips crashed down on hers, taking, giving, coaxing, demanding.

He was right, the time for talking was over. Now was the time for action. She poured her love into every kiss, every touch, every heated moment.

His knees nudged hers apart. "I can't wait any longer."

Neither could she. She pulled her knees up around his waist. "Hurry up, cowboy, I need you."

He nudged her thighs farther apart and sank to the hilt.

A soft sigh whispered from her lips. Yes, this was exactly where they both belonged. She wrapped her legs around him and pulled him deep.

He began to move. At first slowly, languorously, drawing each nerve-tingling second out. But that didn't last long. They were both strung too tight. Slow and languorous gave way to quick and needy, which turned

into a hard and fast pounding that sent them both rock-
eting over the top.

He collapsed on her, his arms tucked beside her so
that most of his weight was supported by his elbows.

She kissed him one more time, drawing his very essence into her as they lay entwined, arms and legs
wrapped around each other. She shivered with pleasure,
their bodies locked intimately, her lips on his, shocks
of pleasure still running through them. Life didn't get
more perfect than this. She pulled her lips from his,
looked into those blue, blue eyes and whispered, "I
love you."

He stilled, the light in his eyes fluttering out. "Don't
go there, Josie."

Her heart clenched. Not the words she'd hoped for,
prayed for. But she wasn't backing down. "I'm already
there," she whispered.

He was standing beside the bed before she had time
to blink, frustration filling his expression. "You said all
you wanted was tonight."

Oh, God. "I lied."

His lips pressed into a hard, angry line. "Well, I
guess we're even then, aren't we?" He picked his briefs
from the pile of clothes and jerked them on.

"It's not the same thing." She scrambled up and retrieved her panties. If he was looking for a quick get-
away, she wanted to be able to run out after him. "You
were just trying to get laid and I was trying to make you
see how much I love you."

He snatched up his jeans. "A lie is a lie, Josie."

"Okay, maybe it is. But my intentions were good. I love you, dang it. And I'm not willing to give up on you just because some other woman hurt you and you're afraid the next one will do the same."

"*That* doesn't have anything to do with my unwillingness to get involved with a woman right now. I told you that. It's about—"

"I know, your son and that stupid million dollars. But it *isn't* about that. It *isn't*. Why won't you see that?" She pulled on her shirt, her heart racing, her fingers too nervous to handle the buttons.

He jerked on his jeans, making quick work of the zipper, but foregoing the snap.

"It's about protecting your heart, Tommy Ray. But I'm not going to hurt you. I *love* you. You. Not what you can give me materialistically. I love *you*. For all the reasons I gave you while we were laying naked in that bed together."

He stilled, his face haunted, his knuckles turning white as he held on to the top of the boot he was pulling on. Finally he blinked, and when he opened his eyes, his expression was closed. He finished pulling on the last boot, stood, stomped it on and grabbed his shirt from the floor. He looked back to her, sadness and regret in those beautiful blue eyes. "I'm sorry. I have to go." He strode out of the room, pulling the door shut behind him.

Josie stood in the middle of the room, her heart aching, tears stinging the back of her eyes. She'd gambled it all.

And lost.

Tommy Ray pounded down the stairs, his heart racing, a cold sweat covering his skin.

Love?

He wasn't going there again. At least not now. Five years, ten years down the road, maybe. But not now.

He pushed out of the house, gulping in the hot, humid air, trying to get enough oxygen into his lungs. When was he going to learn that following that woman upstairs never ended in anything but disaster? He closed his eyes, but he couldn't shut out the image of her face when he'd rolled off her, her disappointment, her hurt.

Damn. He climbed inside his pickup, cranked the engine and sped away from the house. Damn, damn, *damn*. Hurting her was the last thing he'd wanted to do.

He ran a shaky hand down his face. Why couldn't she understand that he needed that million dollars? Why couldn't she see that it wasn't about him?

It was *all* about his son.

Chapter Fourteen

"The next event is the bucking bulls, ladies and gentlemen. Get your wallets out. Pledges will be taken for the next five minutes and then the event begins." The announcement blared over the intercom system.

The sounds of horses, cows and crowds of people filled the air. The smell of popcorn, candy apples and cotton candy tickled the nose. The sun was hot, the crowds were highly jubilant, and the charity was making out like a bandit.

Good. This fund-raiser would make enough money to cover Lily's bills and those of two, possibly even three more people in need. Not bad for a single day's work. But while Josie was thrilled for the charity, her spirits were anything but high.

She made her way through the corrals, dodging horses, cowboys and the masses as nimbly as her fuzzy brain could handle. She hadn't slept since the night Tommy Ray had walked out on her. Between her worry and care for Lily and the ache in her heart, sleep just wouldn't come in any form more extensive than a five-minute catnap. She was tired and clay-headed and…unutterably sad.

She'd known she was taking a risk the other night when she'd brought Tommy Ray up to her room. She'd known she might not be able to push him past his fear of getting involved again. But she hadn't realized how much it would hurt if she lost that battle. She felt as if she'd been flattened by an avalanche. And then had the rescue helicopters land on top of her.

She wasn't sure what difference seeing him would make. He was bound and determined to hide behind his million-dollar goal, but she wanted to see him, anyway. She had one more thought to throw at his head. One more theory she wanted him to think about. Pitiful. But there it was.

She strode into the barn, the musky smell of horses filling her nostrils, the cooler temperature of the covered building a relief from the burning Texas sun. The quiet murmur of male voices came from the other end of the barn, but she couldn't see anyone. Couple of cowboys putting their horses away, no doubt.

Her boots ringing hollowly on the cement aisle, she made her way to the tack room. She was pretty sure she'd left her bull rope there last night. At least she hoped she had. As it happened, bull ropes were as personal as throwing ropes. Every rider did better with the rope that fit him or her the best. And if she was going to make it to the end of her ride, she needed every advantage she could get.

She stepped into the tack room and looked around. It wasn't hanging on the hook she thought she'd left it on. Great. Now what? Maybe she'd put it her tack box. She didn't remember doing so, but her brain wasn't working all that well lately. She checked the box.

And there it was. She grabbed it up and headed back out of the tack room, running smack dab into a big, hard chest. She rocked back on her heels and peered up at the face attached to the muscular wall.

Her heart squeezed. She'd had a million things she was going to say the next time she saw him, but now, her thoughts scattered like so many leaves in the wind. "Hey."

Looking distinctly uneasy, he returned the short greeting with a nod of his head.

The same energy that had sparked to life the first time she'd met him crackled between them, pushing away the daze she'd been in. Her thoughts came back to her, all those questions she wanted to ask. "So where've you been the last few days, cowboy? You abandoned me just before the big event."

He shrugged. "I've been here and at the hospital, just like you. And I didn't abandon you. I sent Trent to help."

"Sending Trent instead of coming yourself is abandoning me. And so is visiting the hospital when you know I won't be there."

He grimaced. "I thought it best—easier—if we didn't run into each other."

"Easier?" There wasn't anything easy about any of this. "Who did you think it was easier for? Me? Or you?"

"Both of us. I thought it was best for both of us."

"Oh, please. It was best for *you.*"

He exhaled a slow breath, his expression unhappy and...dismissive. "It's a dead horse, Josie, let it go. I see you're doing well today. Congratulations."

"How would you possibly know how I'm doing? I haven't seen you anywhere around when I was competing."

"I've been watching the boards. Keeping track."

"Standing on the sidelines again, huh?"

He looked away, his lips pressed into a thin, white line.

"You're a coward, Tommy Ray. Do you know that?"

He hung his hands on his hips, frustration radiating from him like heat from the hard-packed Texas soil. "I don't have time for this. I have an event to get ready for."

She hefted her bull rope. "Me, too. But I have a little time yet. And you ride after me, so... We have time for a little discussion. Have I mentioned I think you're hiding behind your million-dollar goal?"

"Over and over."

"Well, I've discovered yet another layer to that theory."

"I'm thrilled for you." Sarcasm dripped from his words.

"Want to hear it?"

"More than life itself."

"Good. You see, while it was obvious to me you believed you needed that million to be worthy in your son's eyes, I totally overlooked the fact you might *also* believe you needed it to be worthy in the eyes of the next woman you got involved with."

She waited for him to deny it, but the only sound in the barn was that of the announcer barking out the next contestant. Did that mean she was right? Or just that he was ignoring her?

She shook her head, slowly, sadly. "A million dollars won't make your heart safer, Tommy Ray. It might seem that way because Melissa left because you couldn't give her everything she wanted, but there are innumerable other reasons marriages don't work out. And having that financial cushion isn't going to take care of most of them. In the end you're going to have to risk your heart, that's all there is to it."

"Well, I won't have to risk it today, will I?" His tone was short and curt, dismissive as he pushed around her.

"So you're admitting I'm right about all this? That

one of the reasons you want that million is because you think it'll make you more worthy in the eyes of the next Mrs. Bartel?"

"I'm not admitting anything. You wanted to talk. I listened. But I'm done listening now. Like I said, I have an event to get ready for."

"And like *I* said, you're a coward. As soon as things start heating up, you run away."

He didn't rise to the bait, he just opened the cabinet on the other side of the small room and started rummaging through it.

She sighed. "When are you going to figure out that Melissa leaving because you weren't rich enough for her isn't an affront to your character but a statement on hers?"

"Josie."

Josie startled at Nell's voice. She'd been so engrossed in her argument with Tommy Ray, she hadn't heard anyone approaching the tack room. She glanced over her shoulder. "Yeah?"

Nell's gaze slid between Josie and Tommy Ray. "Everything okay?"

Josie almost smiled. Nell was looking out for her, ready to rip poor Tommy Ray apart if he hurt her again. But she didn't need her protection now. She was trying to bring him around, not run him off. "Everything's fine," she reassured.

Nell shot Tommy Ray a warning glance. "Better be." Then she looked back to Josie and tipped her head toward the arena where all the events were taking place. "There's a cowboy riding now, then Crissy is up and then it's you. You need to get to the chutes.

She nodded and tossed her bull rope to her girlfriend. "Have them get my bull ready and tell them I'm coming." She watched Nell disappear. Time to crawl on the bull she'd chosen for her ride. She ran a tired hand down her face, rubbing at her eyes. She might have been better off downing a cup of coffee instead of hammering at Tommy Ray's hard head. But, she'd had to try.

When she turned back to Tommy Ray, he'd quit rummaging in the cabinet. He was watching her. "If you're tired you have no business getting on a bull."

She waved away his concern. "I'm not that tired. And I want to ride. I want Lily to know I'm not afraid to take a risk for her. And I want *you* to know the same thing. I'm dedicating my last ride of the day to you two. And if I don't want to miss it, I'd best get my butt moving." She gave him a nod. "See ya later, cowboy." At least she hoped she did.

Tommy Ray watched her disappear, her words echoing in his head.

Coward.

In the end you're going to have to risk your heart, that's all there is to it.

His heart pounded. His palms sweated. *Is* that what it all boiled down to? Whether or not he was ready to take another chance? Was flat-out fear of getting involved again the driving motivation behind his million-dollar goal?

Footsteps sounded outside the tack room. Damn. He'd forgotten he wasn't alone. Forgotten his daddy had come to the barn with him.

Now the older man stepped into the tack room, a crooked smile on his face. "That's one feisty Angel."

Great. His daddy had obviously been eavesdropping. He ran a hand down his face. "How much did you hear?"

"Enough to know she seems to be as astute as she is feisty."

"*Astute?* You think she's right? You think I'm *afraid* to get involved with another woman? That I'm hiding?"

"You know, son, it doesn't matter what I think. The only thing that matters is what you think. Not what you open your mouth and tell people, but what you believe here." He tapped his chest, right over his heart. "Do you think you're less of a man because you don't have a big wad of cash to back you up?"

"*No.*" The answer came quickly, automatically. But honestly? He wasn't so sure anymore.

And maybe this was the time to be sure.

He started sifting through the thoughts in his head. "To tell the truth, I don't think I know anymore, Daddy. Money *does* matter to a lot of people. I think it will matter to my son."

His father's gaze was sharp, assessing. "And to the next woman you get involved with?"

"It certainly mattered to the last woman I was involved with." He couldn't keep the bitterness from his voice. Or the pain from his heart.

"Yes, it did."

Tommy Ray paced the small, confined space of the tack room. But did he believe money would make a difference to the next woman? "I didn't invent my million-dollar goal so I'd have money for the next woman I got involved with. Nor did I invent it so I would have an excuse *not* to get involved again. Am I using it for that purpose now? I don't know. Maybe. But that goal is legitimate. I *need* that money if I'm ever going to be anything more than a failure in my son's eyes."

Something flashed in his daddy's expression. Striding over to one of the bigger tack trunks, he sat, crossed one leg over the other, set his cowboy hat on his knee and leveled his gaze on Tommy Ray. "You ashamed of me?"

"What?"

"You heard me. Are you ashamed of me?"

"Why on earth would I be ashamed of you?"

"I don't make much money. Never have."

Oh, God, he should have seen this coming. He shook his head adamantly. "Don't even think it, Daddy. You were the perfect father." He had to smile. "Or as perfect as a father gets. An extra hour tacked onto Saturday-night curfew would have been nice. But we never wanted for anything. We always had a roof over our heads and food in our bellies. And your attention. No matter how many extra hours you worked at the mill, trying to make ends meet, you always found time for us. For me. Time to help me with my homework, teach me how to ride a horse, how to tune a car. You were always there for me. And for the other kids, too. We always knew we could count on you, always knew you loved us. *I* always knew. That's what matters."

"But your son needs more than that? Deserves more than that?"

"*No.* It's just..." Damn. "I want it to be the same thing, Daddy. I do. But it's not. Melissa's new husband will be able to give that boy things I can't. Fancy things. The kind of things that turn a kid's head."

"And you're afraid you'll come up a sorry second if you don't have that million?"

"Yes." It was an ugly truth, but it was his.

His father shrugged. "There are things Melissa's husband won't be able to give him that you will. Your heritage for one. Someone's got to teach that boy to ride a horse. Not some fancy froo-froo horse with a silly saddle and shiny hooves. But a real let's-see-if-you-can-keep-your-butt-in-the-saddle-while-I-do-my-job kind of horse. And then there's a good work ethic. He's being raised by two trust-fund babies who never worked a day in their lives. How are they going to teach him the importance of a good work ethic? And as much as I hate to speak ill of my grandson's mother, the word *work* isn't even in her vocabulary. And I doubt it's in her husband's, either."

No, Tommy Ray was pretty sure neither of them knew anything about work, but... "You're missing the point, Daddy. He won't need a good work ethic. He's one of those trust-fund babies himself."

"Yes, he is. But there should be more to a man than his money. He needs a sense of pride in himself. When his days are done, he needs to know he accomplished something on this earth. Something worthwhile. A good work ethic is where that process starts. And Tommy Dean needs you to show him that, because no one else in his life can. The people in his life now don't even know it's required." Disgust sounded in his father's voice.

Of all the pieces of the puzzle that went together to make up his life, this is one piece he hadn't thought of. He sighed. "You might be right. But money is going to complicate this issue, too. Because, like it or not, money is an integral part of the work-ethic equation. Let's say I manage to steal Tommy Dean away for a few months and teach him how to ranch, the only thing I know how to do. Even if he was able to work six months, his pay would probably be less than his monthly allowance. How will he possibly feel like he's doing anything but wasting his time?"

"Because it's *not* about the money, boy."

"Part of it is."

"Not the part that matters," his father insisted. "Do you remember the summer you were thirteen? The summer you spent breaking and training your first green horse?"

"Yes." How could he forget?

"You didn't get paid a red cent for working with that animal. Did you feel like you were wasting your time? Or were you proud of your accomplishment?"

He thought back to that day. To the first time he'd climbed on the big, rawboned horse's back. To the hard, neck-jerking bucks the animal had performed trying to unseat him. He'd hung on for his life, hung on until the hard bucks had turned to easier, crow-hopping ones, and eventually had stopped altogether, leaving the horse to run his anger out in the big corral. It had been a sweet triumph. And by the end of the summer, old Smoke had become a promising young cutting horse. Tommy Ray had felt like a damned king.

And no one knew that better than his daddy. Tommy Ray had been so proud of himself he'd crowed about his accomplishments from dawn until dusk all summer long. He'd been an insufferable ass, and his old man had just smiled proudly, clapped him on the back and told him what a good cowboy he was.

A smile much like the one he'd seen on his father's lips that summer turned the old man's lips now. "So, you see, you *do* have things to contribute to your son's life. Things, in my opinion, that are much more important than the money he'll inherit from his mother and her husband."

Maybe he did.

But, he also knew how powerful the lure of money could be. He'd lost his first marriage to it. The thought of losing his son over it scared him to death. "What if I can't pull it off?"

The old man had the audacity to chuckle. *Chuckle!* "What? You want guarantees? Sorry, you might get them in the next life, but nobody gets them in this one. And you might want to remember that a man is not defined by how he stands by his values and beliefs when his life is going well, but how he stands by them when the odds are stacked against him."

Tommy Ray studied the man sitting on the tack trunk. "You don't think I should be waiting to make that million before I see Tommy Dean, do you?"

"Like I said, doesn't matter what I think. You're a grown man. In charge of your own life. But you might want to remember that while you were reassuring me you're not ashamed of your old man, you pointed out I was always there for you kids. There to support you, guide you, make sure you knew you were loved. How is making that million dollars doing any of that for Tommy Dean?"

A thousand thoughts and fears raced in his head. Had he really misjudged his situation so badly? Was money not important at all? Had he simply lost sight of the values he'd been raised with because Melissa's values weren't the same? Or was money more important that his daddy thought?

He remembered the look on Lily's face the day he'd missed her dialysis appointment. She hadn't given a damn about the pony. And this was a girl who had nothing. She should have been thrilled that he'd brought her such a neat gift. But she hadn't been. What she'd wanted had been his support.

And he had failed her.

A cold fist closed around his gut. He hadn't seen his son for four years. "I might have screwed up here."

"You might have. But you're lucky, there's time for a second chance."

He nodded, trying to picture his son's face, trying to imagine what it would feel like to have the boy in his arms again.

"Now," his daddy went on. "Let's talk about that feisty Angel of yours."

Sweet Josie Quinn.

His heart pounded faster.

She'd been right about a lot of things. She'd been right about his presence being more important than money in Tommy Dean's life. She'd been right about him believing the million would make him more worthy in a woman's eyes. Was she right about the other, too? Was he avoiding relationships not because he had a goal to achieve, but because he was afraid of risking his heart?

He'd barely had time to form the questions when the PA system crackled to life. "Ladies and gentlemen, we have a special treat coming up next. Alpine Angel Josie Quinn has made a special deal with the corporations forking over the big bucks for this fund-raiser. She's convinced them to double their usual reward. That makes ten thousand dollars for every second she stays on her bull. In return she'll be riding the only bull on the pro rodeo circuit never to have been ridden to the bell…the notorious Screaming Jack!"

Fear more potent that he'd ever felt slammed through him. His father's gaze snapped wide. "I thought that bull was banned from the rodeo circuit."

"He was." But this wasn't a pro rodeo-sanctioned event.

And Josie Quinn was one determined woman.

I want Lily to know I'm not afraid to take a risk for her. And I want you to know the same thing. I'm dedicating my last ride of the day to you two.

Dear God.

He spun and raced for the chutes, praying he'd get there before they opened the damned gate.

Chapter Fifteen

He could see the chutes from here, see they were about to open the gate. "Josie! Trent! Don't open that damned gate!" Wasted breath. The crowd was too loud. The only people who heard were the ten people around him. And they were looking at him like he'd lost his mind.

He tried to run harder, faster. But the crowds prevented it. He watched Josie snuggle deeper onto Jack's back. The big, powerful bull lunged upward and snorted—a loud, angry snort as he tried to dislodge his rider, rub her off on the hard metal rails.

He had to get to the chutes.

Now.

He dodged a gang of teens, a family of four and a

couple with a stroller, only to come hard up against a tight crowd surrounding the big corral where the events were taking place.

Damn. He started shoving his way through. "Move. Move. I have to get to the chutes."

His dad was right behind him, doing his own pushing and shoving.

Finally, finally Tommy Ray made it through to the backside of the small pens.

But it was too late.

The gate swung open, and Screaming Jack exploded out of it, bellowing like the lunatic he was. The powerful animal's front feet hit the ground with the force of a pile driver, his back feet slammed toward the sky and his body turned itself inside out as he started the mad bucking that had thrown every cowboy that had ever sat on his back. And most of the best had been there.

Josie had a tight grip on the bull rope, and she was leaning back. Way back. But she was being tossed around like a rag doll. A tiny, fragile, very breakable doll.

Time shifted.

Slowed.

Stopped.

Fear, real fear, grabbed him by the throat—and squeezed. What if he lost her?

A humorless laugh echoed through his head. Five minutes ago he hadn't even known he'd wanted her.

Not true.

He'd wanted her. From the moment he'd first seen her. He'd just been too much of a fool to admit it. Too much of a coward.

Time to change that.

Time snapped back into place. He was straddling the top rail of the corral fence. How the hell had he gotten up here?

Who cared? The only important thing was that he was ready to jump in and help divert the bull's attention from Josie when she went flying. He caught the eye of the pick-up man and pointed toward Josie. "Get over there. Get ready to get her."

As the cowboy trotted closer, Tommy Ray did a quick sweep of the corral rail. The clown was in position to do his job of keeping the bull from going after Josie. Three other cowboys straddled the gate, ready to do the same thing. Good. They knew what they were dealing with and were ready to help.

He looked back to the action in the arena. Jack was bucking for all he was worth, his front end going one way, his back end going the other. The sound of the cheering crowd egged the beast on.

And Josie was still hanging on. A bloody miracle.

One that couldn't last for long. Tommy Ray's heart pounded. A cold sweat covered his skin. As long as she stayed up, she was safe. But once she was on the ground, that's when she'd be in danger.

Four seconds.

His inner clock had started ticking the minute the

gate had swung open. Most cowboys had hit the dust by now. But Josie was still up. Still hanging on. But then she'd been on a mission when she'd climbed on board that crazy son.

I want Lily to know I'm not afraid to take a risk for her. And I want you to know the same thing.

She was hanging on for them. His daddy was right. She was one feisty Angel.

Five seconds.

Son of a buck, she was going to ride to the bell.

Pride—*love*—swelled in his chest.

Six seconds.

The bell sounded.

Thank God. But his relief didn't last for more than a split second. Josie was relaxing. And on Jack, that's all it took. She went flying.

Tommy Ray's feet hit the ground before she did.

The clown and cowboys sprang into action.

But so did Jack. He was already spinning around, looking for his target.

Josie hit the ground hard, her shoulders and neck first. Ouch. He'd had enough experience to know she was seeing stars. And her lack of movement proved it. She was no doubt trying to get her bearings and breath back.

And Jack had her in his sights. With a loud bellow he charged, leading with his long Brahman horns.

Pure terror ripped through Tommy Ray. He had to distract that bull. He hollered as loud as he could.

Jack spun on a heel, amazingly nimble for a big animal. His beady little eyes searched for the source of the yell.

Tommy Ray waved his arms and bellowed even louder. *"Come get me you sorry excuse for a cow."*

Jack bellowed right back. And charged.

Hooves thundered toward him. The crowd breathed in a collective breath. Tommy Ray held his ground, giving the bull a target. At the last second he dodged left. But he wasn't quick enough. Jack caught him with those wide horns and gave his big, hard head a mighty toss.

The sky flashed by, followed by the earth and the sky again. He was sailing high. And now he was headed down. Oh, man this was going to hurt. He consciously relaxed his muscles, preparing to roll with the hit. Preparing to get back on his feet and run.

Gravity slammed him back to earth. His breath whooshed out, pain shot through his hip, but he rolled to his feet. Not as nimbly as Jack—who was changing direction, getting ready for another charge—but he was up. Not two feet from where Josie was starting to come to life. He had to get that bull out of here.

From the corner of his eye he saw a flash of color. The clown moving in, fast and loud.

Jack swung that big, ugly head in the clown's direction and charged.

Tommy Ray quickly snatched Josie up, cradled her in his arms and ran for the rail. His dad was perched on the top rail, holding his arms out. Tommy Ray tossed up Josie and managed to haul his own sorry ass out of the arena just as Jack clanged into the rail below them. That was one crazy bull.

But he wasn't Tommy Ray's problem anymore. He vaulted to the ground on the other side of the fence and held out his arms for Josie.

His dad handed her down.

"I'm okay, I can stand."

He wanted to hold her close, but after the ride she'd given she had every right to stand on her own two feet. He reluctantly set her down. But he couldn't stop from running his gaze anxiously over her, looking for injury. "You sure you're okay?"

She nodded, her breathing becoming steadier and deeper. Her eyes grew sharper and more focused as excitement started to sparkle in them. A smile bloomed on her face. "I made it to the bell."

He could practically see the adrenaline coursing through her. "Yes, you did. Was it fun?"

She nodded, the smile just getting wider and wider.

"Good. Because you're never doing it again." He looked around, spotted what he was looking for—a quiet corner where they could have a private chat. He started dragging Josie toward it.

"Hey, where are we going?"

"Just over here, between the barn and the hay shed. I need to talk to you. Alone."

"Really?" Interest sounded in her voice.

He glanced over his shoulder. "Don't look so excited, you're not going to like all of it." Anger was starting to replace his awe and fear. What the hell had she been thinking, getting on that bull? For any reason.

He pulled her into the small, blessedly empty niche behind the barn and the shed and turned to face her, pinning her with a hard gaze. "What? Did you miss the part about that bull being crazy the day I found you and Lily with him behind the barn?"

She didn't look the least perturbed by his anger. "No. I heard you. And afterward I did some research on him. Found out all about him. That's why I was able to get the corporations to up their ante."

"You did this for *money?* Have you lost your mind?"

She shook her head. "Doing things for money is your thing, remember? I told you why I did it." She locked her gaze on his. "I did it for you and Lily."

"And what did you think Lily was going to do without you if that bull had killed you?"

She went pale. "I didn't think of that. I'm not used to having anyone depend on me, and… Okay, not the best plan. Next time I'll give it a little more thought. But I didn't have time for an elaborate scheme. I wanted Lily to know how important she was. And I needed something bold to catch your attention." She licked her lips, clearly nervous about pushing on. But push on she did. "How'd I do?"

He pictured her being tossed around on the damned bull. He closed the distance between them until he was towering over her. "In the future, you want my attention, I'd recommend something a little more subtle, terror tactics will not be looked upon favorably."

Hope flickered to life in her expression. "In the future? Does that mean you're thinking about a future…for us?" Her words were soft, breathy, as if she was afraid to say them.

The moment of truth was upon him. He drew a deep breath and met her gaze head-on. "Yes."

"Yes?" More hope grew in those angel eyes.

"As much as it pains me to say it, you were right about all of it. I *was* afraid. But I'm done playing from the sidelines. My son does need me more than he needs that million dollars. And—"

"And how did you finally figure that out, if you don't mind my asking?"

"You can't just take my word for it that it's true? You have to hear all the details?"

She took his hand—no doubt to keep him from running away—and smiled sweetly at him. "Hey, communication is a good thing."

Like most of the males on this planet, he wasn't so sure. But she'd ridden the notorious Screaming Jack for him. He owed her. "You got me started."

"Maybe. But I didn't convince you."

"No. Something my daddy said did that."

"What did he say?"

"He asked me if I was ashamed of him."

Her eyes went wide. "Ashamed of him? Why on earth would you be ashamed of your dad?"

He chuckled. "My words exactly. But he was quick to point out he wasn't rich, never had been."

"And it didn't matter, did it?"

He let out his breath. Josie understood. She'd understood all along. "When I was growing up, money wasn't important. Would it have been nice to have? You bet. But would I have traded my daddy's love and support for a big bank account. Never."

"But that's what you've been asking your son to do."

"Not anymore. I'll be calling his mom tonight, letting her know she'd best get used to me being in Tommy Dean's life."

She squeezed his hands, her expression softening. "Good for you."

"Yeah, good for me." He smiled down at her. "You want to hear the other big revelation?"

She shot him a cheeky grin. "More than life itself."

He had to laugh. But then he turned serious. "It hurt like hell when I lost my family. My wife. My son. I didn't ever want to feel that way again."

She looked into his eyes and ran a finger gently along his jaw. "I'm not going to make you feel that way, Tommy Ray. I love you."

"Thank God, because for all my efforts, both conscious and unconscious, to protect my heart, at some point when I wasn't looking, it snuck away. Jumped right in your back pocket."

Moisture gathered in her eyes and she cuddled close, bumping his hips with hers. "Is that right?"

He stared down at her face. Her dear, dear face. Those full, mouthwatering, kiss-me lips. Those soft angel eyes. His wholesome love goddess through and through. "I love you, Josie Quinn. I want to help you build the home you've always dreamed of. Give you the family you've always wanted." He caught her left hand and gently rubbed the top of her fourth finger. "And I want to put a ring on this finger as quickly as I can get it there."

She chuckled, low and sexy. "What can I say, you gotta love a man who knows what he wants."

Hope blossomed in his own chest. "Is that a yes?"

She wrapped her arms around his neck and stared up at him, joy and happy tears sparkling in her eyes. "A great big, Texas-size yes, cowboy. Now kiss me."

He lowered his lips to hers, kissing her softly, sweetly and with every ounce of love in his heart.

She opened her mouth to his, taking him in. Bringing him home.

Epilogue

The sound of steel guitars drifted up to the bedroom in the big house. The wedding reception was still going strong. Would probably still be going strong at midnight. Nobody appreciated a good party like a Texan.

Josie laid her wedding dress on the bed, carefully arranging the yards of lace. After she and Tommy Ray and Lily left, Mattie would have the beautiful gown cleaned and stored for the next generation.

Josie smiled. Mattie had helped some with Crissy's nuptials, but she'd handled practically everything for Josie's wedding. The flowers, the food, the music. She'd been a godsend because Josie's hands had been full with moving her stuff from Colorado, planning the work that would soon start on the barn and getting Lily on her feet.

She and Tommy Ray could have pushed the wedding back, of course, but they hadn't wanted to. They'd wanted to become a family as quickly as possible. The only thing they'd stalled for was Lily's health.

Josie straightened one final stretch of lace and shifted her gaze to Tommy Ray. A love so deep it hurt squeezed her heart. She was the luckiest woman alive to find a man as loving and giving as Tommy Ray Bartel. She watched him pull on a pair of jeans, his chest still gloriously naked. Heat and need shivered through her. Add sexy to that list.

He caught her staring. His hands froze on his zipper, desire filling his expression. "Should I take these off? We could steal ten minutes before we go back down."

A loud banging on the connecting door sliced through the sexual tension. "Aren't you guys ready yet?" Lily hollered through the door.

Tommy Ray chuckled, finishing up with the zipper and snapping the snap. "Rain check?"

"You bet." She strode over to him, gave him a deep kiss, letting their love and desire slide between them before pulling her lips from his and moving to the connecting door and unlocking it.

Lily bounced in, carrying the small overnight case Josie had helped her pack earlier. "Come on, let's go." She looked up at Tommy Ray. "I want to show Mom the 'sprise."

"Lily," Tommy Ray said, obviously trying to shush the child.

Josie shot Tommy Ray a questioning look. "There's a surprise?"

"A big one. Come on." Lily grabbed her hand and started pulling.

Tommy Ray chuckled at Lily's lack of subterfuge. "You have to wait until I'm dressed, squirt."

"Well, *hurry* then. I want to show her." She bounced on her toes, her hand wrapped tight around Josie's.

Josie narrowed her eyes on the two conspirators. "What do you two have up your sleeves?"

Tommy Ray smiled secretively. "You'll see." He made quick work of putting on his shirt, a pair of socks and his boots, then made his way to the dresser, took something out of the top drawer and slid it into his front pocket. "Okay, let's go."

Josie took a last look around the room, making sure one of them hadn't left something they'd need on their trip. "The luggage is already in the car, right?"

Lily giggled.

Tommy Ray's secretive smile got a little wider. "Yep. Let's go."

What were they up to? Josie grabbed her purse as Lily pulled her out of the room and down the stairs to the great room where the reception was still underway. As soon as they hit the end of the landing, the Angels and Tommy Ray's family gathered around them.

A sense of peace and belonging enveloped Josie.

Tommy Ray's family had made it clear from the moment Tommy Ray had announced their engagement that they considered her one of the family. Tears stung her eyes. She'd come to the Big T wondering if she was about to lose the only family she'd ever had. And now, not only were her ties to Crissy stronger, but she had another family, as well. A big, gregarious, loving family.

Had she mentioned she was the luckiest girl alive?

Nancy gave the new Bartel family a collective hug, then looked to Josie and Tommy Ray. "You have your tickets?"

Josie lifted her purse. "Madrid, Spain, here we come."

Tears sparkled in Nancy's eyes. "You have your digital camera? You're going to send us pictures right away?"

"You bet."

Lily rose up on her toes, cupping her hands around her mouth. "We're going to visit my *brother* there."

Nancy chuckled. "Yes, you are. And I want to see lots of pictures of you two together."

"There aren't going to be any pictures at all if you three don't get going," Crissy worried. "Your plane leaves in three hours."

"You're right, we'd better hurry." Josie threw her arms around Crissy, giving her a giant hug.

Nell and Mattie joined the group, the Angels wishing her love and happiness.

With a final hug Crissy stepped back and looked to

Tommy Ray, her expression serious as she indicated Josie and Lily. "You better take care of these two."

Tommy Ray put one arm around Josie and a hand on Lily's shoulder, pulling them both tight. "I intend to."

Crissy nodded. "Good."

"Come *on*," Lily piped up. "I want to show Mom the 'sprise." She started pulling Josie toward the front door.

Josie glanced over her shoulder at Tommy Ray. "You two have been conspiring against me."

Tommy Ray gave her that heart-stopping smile. "Yeah, but you're going to love it."

They all made their way out to the front porch.

And there, sitting proudly on the other side of the railing, sat the Biarritz, as fresh-looking as the day she'd first rolled off the assembly line, her new paint sparkling in the sun.

Josie snapped her gaze to Tommy Ray, excitement fizzing in her veins. "*Pink? You painted her pink?*"

He fished in his front pocket, the one he'd put something in earlier, pulled out a set of keys and dangled them in front of her. "Would you have wanted any other color?"

"Mine?" she squeaked.

He took her hand, placed the keys in it. "For the woman who lassoed my heart. Ready to take her for a spin?"

"Yeah! Come on." Lily jumped off the porch.

Josie chuckled. "I'm with Lily on this one. Let's get going." She couldn't wait to drive that car.

They said their final goodbyes, buckled Lily into the back seat and climbed into the front.

Josie ran her hands over the leather upholstery, the original plastic steering wheel. She looked over at Tommy Ray, her heart bursting with joy. "A pink Cadillac, the man of my dreams and the perfect little family. I don't think life gets any better than this."

He smiled back. "It is perfect. Although, a night to celebrate, just me and you, might have been nice." Desire burned in those blue, blue eyes. Desire and a hint of apology.

She reached across the car and gave his hand a squeeze. "Hey, we're going to have those nights. Lots and lots of them. But we have one more member of this family to claim, and I'm as anxious for that as you."

"Then let's go get him, for pity's sake," Lily said from the back seat. "This lovey-dovey stuff is just slowing us down."

They both laughed. "Okay, okay, I'm going," Josie said, turning the ignition and heading down the road. She looked back to Tommy Ray, taking in that handsome cowboy face. "You excited about little Tommy?"

He smiled over at her. "I can't tell you."

"You don't have to. I can see it in your face." She was staring at the sexiest smile this side of the Rio Grande—and the happiest eyes she'd ever seen.

* * * * *

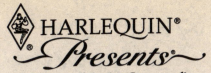

HARLEQUIN®
Presents

Seduction and Passion Guaranteed!

They're the men who have everything—
except brides…

Wealth, power, charm—what else could a
heart-stoppingly handsome tycoon need?
In the GREEK TYCOONS miniseries you have
already been introduced to some gorgeous Greek
multimillionaires who are in need of wives.

**Now it's the turn of favorite Presents
author Lucy Monroe,
with her attention-grabbing romance**

THE GREEK'S INNOCENT VIRGIN
Coming in May
#2464

If you enjoyed what you just read,
then we've got an offer you can't resist!

Take 2 bestselling love stories FREE!
Plus get a FREE surprise gift!

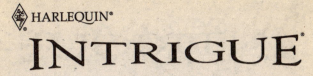

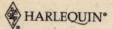